BROTHERHOOD

BROTHERHOOD
A WESTERN DOUBLE

LEVI JOHNSON MOUNTAIN MAN SCOUT
BOOK FOUR

ASH LINGAM

WOLFPACK
PUBLISHING
— EST 2013 —

Brotherhood
Paperback Edition
Copyright © 2025 (As Revised) by Ash Lingam

Wolfpack Publishing
1707 E. Diana Street
Tampa, Florida 33610

www.wolfpackpublishing.com

Paperback ISBN 979-8-89567-234-1
Ebook ISBN 979-8-89567-233-4

CONTENTS

BROTHERHOOD

THE JOURNEY

BROTHERHOOD

BROTHERHOOD

LEVI JOHNSON MOUNTAIN MAN
SCOUT 7

Good moral character is the first essential in a man.

George Washington

FIRST SNOW

THE RIDER RODE A BEAUTIFUL BLACK STALLION AND SAT atop the animal like he was ready to take on the world. His saddle and horse bore the brands of USC—the United States Cavalry. Confidence oozed from the man even from a distance. He wore Army boots, britches, and a shirt with a Seventh Cavalry hat slapped up on the side. A long saber hung from his belt. His flowing blond hair hung below his shoulders and fluttered in the wind as his horse walked through the crisp snow.

Not another track was visible. Breaths of horse and rider could be seen as they climbed the mountain, and the temperatures dropped. He was obviously an officer, but his rank under his bearskin coat was hard to tell. It hung open so he could quickly get to his pistols.

A mule followed behind, loaded with supplies. The rider wore a week's stubble, and the first wrinkles appeared on his face beside small battle scars. He pulled off his hat and used it to block the sun and gaze into the distance with his cat-green eyes. Traces of gray showed at his temples. He didn't know exactly where he was going but had followed the tales as he traveled. He didn't believe it would be much longer, but it didn't matter if it was. He had no plan of turning back, no matter what the weather or the hostiles did to deter him.

The major had more determination than any man he'd ever met. Now, he felt he had one last thing to do before he was killed in battle or retired, and he wouldn't stop for anybody. Only then would he return to his command and the frontier forts and eventually back home, where he would make his final decision on his future. Would he continue in the Army after all he had seen and done, albeit while following orders?

Of course, all that depended on whether he survived his current journey and returned to his posting. It was always possible that the brass wouldn't agree with him and made him stay on the front line of the Indian wars. He had been there too long, and there wasn't a man left alive from when he arrived. He felt that if he stayed longer, he wouldn't survive either. He had been in the south fighting Comanche and had scars from wounds to prove it.

He still couldn't understand how uneducated people could have such cunning in warfare. They were unbeatable up till now. They could fire more arrows than the soldiers could shoot bullets. The Comanche prided themselves in shooting four arrows in three seconds. They stuck them between their fingers and fired them so fast it was a blurred motion. What he had seen them do to White men and what White men had done to them left him scared, not only outside, but inside, too.

The major was a torn and damaged man. He had spent many months fighting Comanche on the

Southern Plains south of the Red River. Now that he thought back on it, it'd been over a year. Buffalo Hump and a massive war party of five thousand warriors had assembled. They had gone on the warpath, and they had fought them touch and go all the way across the state. After they burned Linnville, the second largest port in Texas, Buffalo Hump, Yellow Wolf, and Santa Anna ransacked the town of Victoria and stole thousands of horses. Afterward, they tried to take the herd with them back to West Texas and their hidden camps.

With the Army on their tails, they lost most of the animals during their retreat, and many men on both sides died—many more than should have. The Indians were fighting to protect their land and families. The White men were fighting for their greed for land. There was a big difference between the two. They kept expecting the tides to change, but they were outgunned with crude weapons. What he had seen and the orders he'd been given turned his stomach. He now found himself at the end of his rope. He didn't know if he could continue with the Army like the rest of his family or go home and become a merchant or adopt some simple man's life.

He knew it would take a long time for him to heal from what he had seen and even done. Of course, as an officer, he'd participated in the massacres even though he only followed orders. And to disobey an order in times of war, even though they were only the Indian wars, would bring a court-martial and possibly even a firing squad. So he had done his duty and followed orders, but it had left scars so deep they would never heal.

That wasn't an excuse, and he knew it. At the end of

the day, there were no excuses for what he did or felt he had to do. The truth was, nobody could make a man kill innocent women, elders, and children. What was happening in the secrecy of the plains was genocide, clear and simple. There was no other word for it, and the major had had enough, at least enough of the frontier and their forts.

He knew the only way to save his soul was to head back East and be the officer of an inactive command with little responsibility. He had paid his dues ten times over. The Army owed him that much, but he knew better than to trust the Army to comply with their promises. Not only to the poor Native American Indian tribes but even to his soldiers. These things the major told himself to make excuse for his wicked deeds.

Not only had he sent men to their deaths, but he had also ordered them to do the unspeakable. Still, he was an Army major, and despite the tragedy he had witnessed, he was a soldier through and through. He just didn't see things like the brass at the top did. What a mere cavalry major felt was immaterial to them anyway. He had sent reports back to Washington of the state of things on the front lines, which was sickening—not to mention the apparent mass slaughter of the buffalo.

But no one cared enough even to answer his requests, and now he really didn't care anymore, either —he didn't even notice how he was changing. Washington had sent orders to protect all the buffalo hunters and aid them in any way. Washington wanted to speed up the process and kill off the food sources of the natives and deprive them of materials to build their homes. They intended to force them to live a life of the White man's choosing or perish in the process.

The major was at a historical crossroads in his life. He'd had a big-shot send-off when he came West to the frontier forts. Everybody expected great things from him. He was a soldier's soldier. Nobody suspected his current real intentions. Of course, he was an excellent officer and a terror in battle. He'd survived many encounters with hostile Indians. He rode with the reins in his left hand and a pistol grip in his right, ever ready to fight.

He had seen the elephant time after time and had survived. Now, he had gone off the grid to deal with a personal matter. His green eyes flashed, but he saw nothing but more snow in the distance. Maybe he was going the wrong way.

Despite the doubt, he trudged on. Often, he had to lead both the horse and mule on foot as the trail got too narrow and, in some places, had drop-offs that could easily kill man or beast. The going was getting rougher as he climbed higher.

"How bad could it get?" he asked himself. "Not any worse than what I've already seen and done."

If the truth be known, at times, he had even contemplated suicide. The nightmares stayed with him almost every night and were so real he had to experience time after time what he had done. It was slowly driving him crazy. It wasn't until he decided to make this journey that his mind found some small respite from his torment, and he could focus on something other than the sins he had committed against mankind and the Almighty.

The major squinted as the sun reflected off the fresh

coat of snow. The icy surface crunched with each hoof step. The stocks of two long rifles protruded from leather sheaths on either side of the horse. The animal's muscles rippled when it moved. All the soldier could do was stop it from breaking into a run. Horses weren't as surefooted as mules, but the major felt that to ride such an animal was beneath him and his rank. How could he lead an attack against an enemy on a mule? Even though it was probably the preferred animal for such terrain, he felt that their only use was to carry his supplies. How could he ride into battle on the back of a jackass?

He rode as proud as an Indian warrior. Four flint-lock pistols stuck from his belt. He dared any man to stop him. He had a mission to accomplish, and nothing in this world was going to stop him. He had been warned about the hostile Indians and the winter weather but couldn't help himself. He had to find out the truth; if it meant testing his limitations, so be it. He kept his eyes forward but took everything in with his peripheral vision.

He, like all hunters, sought out his prey by motion. He took mental note of all the places hostile Indians could attack and constantly listened for out-of-place noises. He had been fighting Indian warriors on the run for weeks and weeks. The state of mind he was in wasn't something you could flip a switch and turn off or on. It would take some time for the inherent violence to disappear slowly. What would be left afterward remained to be seen.

He had six bullets and a saber, so he felt he could stifle an attack from a small war party. He also knew most people didn't travel far in the Rocky Mountains during the winter, so he expected to find light resistance and see few humans. His black stallion began to buck, and he struggled with the powerful animal. It sensed something as it reared and kicked its front hooves in the air.

The officer dismounted his horse and grabbed his head and wrestled him to the ground. He lay on the horse's neck, pulled his Springfield, and cocked the hammer. He knew somebody was out there, and he doubted they were friendly. The pack mule ran up the trail like its tail was on fire.

His horse continued to struggle and kick. In less than a minute, the major saw what the horse had smelled. The grizzly bear lumbered out of the dense brush and onto the trail. He was upwind and looking the other way. But the major knew the wind could shift or his horse could make a sound despite its training, and the bear would be on them. He couldn't turn and run on the narrow, slippery trail.

The cavalryman pulled his Springfield and took a bead but held his fire. He wanted to see if the bear turned or not. He wasn't sure one shot could kill such a massive animal. As he waited, he broke out in a sweat and beads of perspiration rolled down the sides of his face. He held his breath as he waited. Then his horse squealed, and he waited for the monster to turn so he had a better chance of hitting its heart.

A boom sounded, the rifle recoiled, and a lead slug roared out the barrel, racing through the air at supersonic speed. It hit the bear like a sledgehammer. Still, it didn't go down. But the slug did stop the grizzly in mid-stride. He batted at the hole in his chest like it was a fly. Blood pumped out with each beat of its heart. It took one wobbly step forward, then another. The major sighed a long sigh, and suddenly the bear took another breath and roared like nothing the soldier had ever seen or heard.

His heart nearly stopped as it lunged forward. It fell on the major like a ton of bricks, as he waited for certain death. It huffed in his ear—it was so close its breath was hot on the major's neck. He began to say the Lord's Prayer when he just as suddenly heard the bear give a ragged, pain-racked last breath, and its heart stopped. The bear had him pinned down, but it only fell on half his body. He shivered at how close he had come to perishing at the feet of the animal he had just killed. When he moved, he touched its nose with his cheek. A shiver crawled up his spine.

He pushed the head aside and wiggled his legs out from under the massive grizzly bear. The major jumped to his feet, grabbed his rifle, and began to reload as his eyes darted all around. His horse jumped to its feet and ran up the trail after the mule; only God knew where it had gone.

He whistled for his horse, but it didn't come. The animal had never smelled a grizzly bear before, and it was as terrifying for the animals as it was for the Army officer. When it didn't come, he walked up the trail and away from the bear. The horse didn't want to get close even though it was dead. That mattered little to the stallion. The major slowly coaxed his animal back to him and grabbed the reins. Then he stepped up, threw his leg over the saddle, and ran down the mule. Lucky for him, nobody had heard the shot, or if they had, they had yet to show their faces.

LEVI JOHNSON and Will Forrester were riding down the mountain. The first winter snow had fallen, and beaver trapping season had begun. They each had a mule behind them piled high with beaver. These wouldn't be the heavy-furred pelts they would acquire further along into the winter. They had been taking traps on each venture deeper into the wilderness and had over twenty set and baited, and the traps were supplying them with a payload of furs.

Forging deeper into the wilderness, Levi, the pathfinder, had found a sizable spring with many creeks flowing from it. It appeared to be a virgin area with no signs of Indian traps, and it was heavy with beaver dams. For so early in the season, they already had half the beaver they had caught last fall. By the time the beaver grew their cold weather pelts, they would be thick and soft for the market.

Levi had decided to trap each spring a different month, always making sure he didn't trap them out. Like all the animals in the wilderness, the hunters had encroached on nearly all areas, resulting in less game. Buffalo hunters came in more significant numbers all the time and now traveled in groups too big for war parties to attack. They, too, killed lots of elk because of their exquisite taste. This, too, was a staple of the American Indian diet. Everyone who could see the big picture knew that a time would come when there wouldn't be enough to go around, and that time wouldn't be as distant as some believed.

They would have to carefully plan the quantity of

what they hunted and trapped to ensure they had a solid supply of food and pelts in the years to come. Too many trappers came to the mountains thinking about the small picture. All they were interested in was making as much money as possible as quickly as they could, and they never considered the game running out and becoming extinct. Of course, it was hard to believe they could ever kill all the buffalo or the grizzlies. They were so densely populated that there seemed to be an endless supply, although most that watched the animals massacred by the tens of thousands wondered how long it could last.

For thousands of years, the North American Indians lived off the more than fifty million bison that roamed the plains. During all that time, the delicate balance of nature was never threatened. Just a few years after White men arrived, their world began to change, and there would never be a possibility of repairing the damage done.

By now, Levi was as good a frontiersman as Rusty Steel. Even Will was beginning to change into the type of person who lived in such a place. Everybody had a choice to leave if they wanted, but these men planned to stay until they were run off or died of natural causes. Will rode behind Levi because he was better at spotting trouble or more game. The man was a natural-born hunter. Although missing his right arm, Will had learned to live without it, and his renewed determination led him to be twice the man he'd been with his appendage.

Now, he understood values he never knew existed in the Army. At this point, it seemed to be a long way away. His new life suited him right down to his boots. He was becoming more like Levi with each passing day. He was sharp as a thorn and picked things up quickly. He was always looking for things to learn. Rusty Steel had schooled them on the plants in that part of the Rocky Mountains. He'd showed them how to dig pine nuts from the cones, what roots cured what ailment, and which plants were poisonous if eaten.

"Do you reckon I'll ever know as much as Rusty?" Will asked. "Every time I think I've learned it all, I find a whole new world has opened up, and I have to start all over again. I try to be as good as you at spotting Indians or game, but it doesn't come as easy to me."

"That's just because you were raised with curtains." Levi laughed. "I grew up in a log cabin in the forest by a river, and I've hunted as far back as I can remember, so it's easier for me. But don't you believe for a minute that I know more than Rusty Steel. He lived with the Indians. I reckon that makes all the difference. Could you imagine growing up with the Comanche? I've never seen any Indians as scary as them."

Just talking about Indians made both men stop talking, and they had a close look around them. They suspected that some of the Crow from the camp often had an eye on them.

"Stop talking about Indians," Will said. "When Rusty's along, I figure if we run into a bunch of Crow, they'll know him, but they may not know us and think we're more trespassers. They're getting very touchy about stepping on their ground without permission. Then again, you can't blame them."

"I doubt there's an Indian one that doesn't know exactly who we are and who we live with." Levi laughed. He seemed to take the Indians in stride—unless they were Comanche. "Don't worry about the Crow, as close as Rusty is with Hachta, and him being the new chief and all; they won't give us no grief. Now, if you spot some Blackfeet Indians, it's another story. They sure as the dickens don't like White people, but they don't like Crow, Sioux, or Ute either."

"It was a stroke of luck finding that other spring and all the creeks that branch from it," Forrester said. "None of the dams were too big, but there sure are a lot of them. I think by Christmas, we'll have a good stock of beaver for next summer and the Rendezvous."

"That's a whole winter away from us, pard," Levi said. "In the wilderness, it's best not to plan too far ahead. It's bad luck. I try to focus on the moment, and then you usually won't miss anything you shouldn't have."

RUSTY STEEL

"ANGUS!" RUSTY SHOUTED FROM THE PORCH. "WHERE'D ya have to go to get that coffee—South America? Iffin I'd have known you were gonna grow your own coffee beans, I'd have made it myself."

"It's my turn to be cook just like it was your turn yesterday," Angus retorted. "I don't remember your salted pork and beans bein' all that special, and your coffee was cold. Mine might take a spell longer, but at least it'll be hot."

"Well, hurry up before my fingers freeze," Rusty complained. "You know I use my hot cup to keep my rheumatism at bay. My fingers don't like the cold no more."

"That's what comes from all these years standing waist deep in freezing water settin' traps. You've near lost half those fingers more than once, and that's just since I've known ya."

"I wonder how those two young mountain men are farin'." Rusty laughed. "I'd give my right arm to have a birds-eye-view of 'em strugglin' to find new ground for beaver. We've been up here a long time, and I doubt two young whippersnappers like them are gonna find what we didn't. I love to watch 'em try, though."

"You don't give Levi credit where credit's due, you old fool." Angus chuckled. "Levi is already as good as you with most things exceptin' lyin' and telling tall tales. In those two categories, I doubt he'll ever beat cha." Angus cackled like an old hen.

Both men were working on stacks of beaver skins. This was what they would do during much of the winter. Especially now that they had two young men eager to learn and weather the cold for them.

"Yes, sir," Angus added. "Now we've got those two young fellas to freeze to death instead of us, life may become easier. Levi sure did a job on the firewood. I thought he was gonna chop down the whole danged forest. We're gettin' too old for such things. Just talkin' about it makes me wanna go see Green Leaves and cuddle up under a warm bear skin in her teepee."

Angus McFarlin poured a cup of coffee for Rusty and another for himself. Steam rose from the tin vessels as Steel wrapped his fingers around the hot tin. It was early morning, and despite the cold, both mountain men sat on the porch and watched the sun climb into the sky from behind the highest peaks. They wore heavy bearskin robes, and their bodies began to heat up with the coffee. Rusty forked a biscuit with a slab of bacon in the middle and said with a mouth full, "I wonder if they found new places to trap? It's gonna take some luck."

"They better have, or we might not be making the money we did last year," Angus said. "We have a bit put away for a rainy day, but we didn't get as rich as we thought we were back at the Rendezvous, now did we? Once the earnings were split up six ways, we've got enough for the new weapons and a little left over for next spring. The Crow have seen how much the pelts are worth, and even though Hachta don't like his men going to the gathering because of the liquor, he has to sell them someplace. The other trappers won't give them a fair deal, and we can't compete against ourselves. I reckon he'll be trapping in some of our creeks and streams pretty soon. Maybe Mister Johnson has found a new hunting ground for us."

"Levi is a clever one, and Forrester is comin' along just fine," Rusty said. "When they first came up here with us, I never thought Will would make it a month. I only let 'im come along because of Beaver Johnson. I reckon that rascal will outshoot me and all in the competition next year."

"I do believe Forrester had to lose that arm to have a clear look at life," Angus said. "That boy had his head stuck up his butt when he first arrived. I figure we buried a lot of problems for that young man when we buried his arm. You give him time, and he'll come along just like Levi. They're both young enough to be hungry for adventure."

"You buried it?" Rusty asked, surprised. "The arm, I mean."

"What else was I supposed to do with it?" Angus asked. "I couldn't leave it for the critters."

Mountain Dennis came walking their way from his cabin next door. He grinned like a possum, making his gold teeth sparkle in the sunlight. It reflected off the ice-covered snow. There were three houses in the compound where six men lived, along with a stables and corral. Now, with the addition of the two young mountain man wannabes, they had eight mouths to feed.

"Mornin', boys," Dennis said as he eyed the coffee pot.

"Go on inside and get yourself a cup," Angus said grumpily. "I ain't gettin' up again until I finish my breakfast. Had ya come on time, you'd have had something to eat like us."

"Where's Sam, Pete, and Bob?" Rusty asked.

"Oh, they'll be along shortly," Dennis replied. "This is the first cold morning, and they're havin' a hard time gettin' out from under their buffalo skins."

"Why, this ain't cold." Rusty snickered. "I've seen the odd summer colder than this."

Dennis sipped his coffee, but he wrinkled his nose. He set the cup down and took another whiff.

"Now I bet you're gonna tell me how bad my coffee is, too," Angus grumbled. "Iffin y'all don't like it, you can make your own."

"No, that ain't it," Dennis said. "I very well know the smell of your horrible coffee, Angus. It's just that I think I smelt something else." He sniffed the air like an old bloodhound. "I smell fancy soap like civilized White folks use. I'd say in an hour we're gonna have company."

"Don't tell me that now you claim to smell a man four or five miles away?" Rusty growled. "You're so full of yourself you don't think your poop stinks."

"Maybe it's the wind that's carryin' the aroma, but that's fancy store-bought soap as sure as we're sittin' here," Dennis said.

"Hogwash," Rusty spat. "There ain't a man alive that can smell that far—not even a Comanche Indian."

Angus laughed. He always found the constant bickering from Rusty Steel and everybody he met entertaining. He often egged him on just to see what he'd do.

"I betcha a gold coin I ain't mistaken," Dennis said.

"And how are ya gonna prove it?" Rusty asked. "Just because you smell somebody, or at least think you do, how do you know he's comin' here? Or maybe it's a bunch of folks all soaped up for us." He laughed.

"Since that there is the main trail up to our cabins, I reckon whoever it is, is on our path," Dennis said. "Where else would he be goin' if not here?"

"Whatcha mean, he's comin' here?" Rusty asked. "Now why would anybody in their right mind come here this time of year? You still ain't proven he's coming at all, fool. If your big nose is so danged good, where're the boys? When are they gonna ride in, mister know-it-all?"

"They be upwind." Dennis grinned. "If the breeze swings around, I'll let cha know when they'll be riding in." He had a devilish twinkle in his eyes.

It was obvious Dennis was playing with Rusty, but Angus had no idea if he was just kidding or not. He knew Breed had a heck of a nose, but that did seem to be a stretch. It was easy to wind Rusty up, though, and they passed their time hacking on each other. Angus sat back and chuckled as they bickered. He refilled the cups as the other three that shared the compound came walking through the snow, packing down a path between the cabins.

They, too, wore bear skin coats and fur boots. But their coats were open, and they weren't wearing hats. It was a little cold with the first snow, but for what was to come, this was hardly the beginning of winter. In a month, the cabin door would be half buried in the snow some mornings. A massive wood pile was stacked beside the side door of each cabin. Levi had cut wood for all three for the long winter to come. The six-foot-seven, 225-pound mountain man chopped firewood like most men whittled sticks.

They could hear the horse ninny and the mule protest to the last bit of steep trail before they could see who it was. Somebody was heading for their compound. Guns lay on the table. Rusty cocked the two nearest him. Dennis was right, though. Now, they could all smell the scented soap. When he rode into view, they were still surprised. They'd expected another trapper but not a soldier on a fancy horse. He rode into the compound like he owned it. That was something that nobody did. He quickly found himself staring down several pistol barrels. The mountain men didn't look welcoming. Their mouths were no more than gashes, and their eyes were hostile. The click of hammers was loud in the still morning. The stallion snorted and stomped its front hooves.

Every time the Army showed up in the mountains, there was trouble with the Indians. Usually, that trouble was caused by the soldiers. Even though he was the only one, they didn't know if he had a patrol below waiting on his orders. Usually, when the Army showed up there on the mountain, they were up to no good, as far as the mountain men could see. Dennis could smell the strong perfumed soap but couldn't smell how many men used it.

"Stop where you are, mister," Rusty growled with a pistol in each mitt. He pointed the barrels at the man on the fancy horse. "Pardon my poor manners, but every time the Army shows up here, we have nothin' but problems. There's a Crow tribe just a few hours from here. Maybe you best get back down that trail before they catch wind you're here. They don't take kindly to Army sorts."

Despite the fact they told him to stop where he was and turn around and leave, he rode his horse to the hitching rail, kicked his boot over his horn, and slid to the ground. Icy snow crunched under his black boots. He casually slapped the reins around the rail. He acted like they hadn't even addressed him. He removed his slapped-up hat, raked his fingers through his hair, and wiped the sweat from his brow with his sleeve. He looked like he was evaluating the men on the porch.

"Whatcha think you're looking at, fool?" Rusty spat.

The officer ignored Steel, looked at Angus, and politely asked, "You wouldn't have another cup of that hot java, would you? I'd be mighty obliged. It might take this chill I got off." Rich coffee rode on the breaths of air. "It gets into my bones."

None of the six weathered mountain men knew what to do. Nobody had ever entered their compound, had guns pointed at them, and completely ignored the guns and the danger. He either didn't see them or was as crazy as a loon.

Angus was so surprised he meekly said, "Hold on a minute, and I'll take care of ya." He brought out a fresh pot and another cup. He placed the gallon kettle on the table.

"Now you've gone and impressed us by not bein' afraid of us with our guns out and all," Rusty said. He was obviously aggravated that the soldier didn't respond to his barking. "So, tell us what it is you're doin' in our compound? Especially as you weren't invited. Where did you get those manners anyway?"

"Are you always so inhospitable?" The major smiled.

A spark of humor twinkled in his eye. What he wasn't was scared like most people who encountered so many onery mountain men. They didn't have the most endearing reputations.

As the sun quickly warmed the morning, the soldier removed his bearskin coat and lay it over his Army-issue saddle.

"Well," the stranger said slowly. "I've been lookin' for somebody—sort of a friend."

"Well, you best keep lookin'," Rusty said. "I don't see any friends of yours around here, and I personally have never seen ya in my life. So, take yourself and mosey on along the trial. I don't give a dang if you go up the trail or back down. Just don't come back this way because strangers ain't welcome this time of year. Winter strangers always bring problems."

The mountain men knew what a major looked like, but Army rank didn't impress them in the wilderness. Not even top-notch soldiers could endure such a place as the Rocky Mountains. It took much more than what they trained you in boot camp and officers' school.

"I swear," Rusty spat. "Here, we build our homes in the middle of nowhere, and it turns out we've got more traffic than the Oregon Trail."

The rusty metal on the weathervane on top of Dennis's cabin screeched when the wind changed direction and swung around a hundred eighty degrees. Dennis sniffed the air again as the officer looked at him, clearly curious. He had a slight smile on his lips, like he found this all amusing.

"Here come the boys," Dennis said to Rusty in a low voice, but the soldier caught it just the same.

He seemed amused and clearly wasn't scared of six woolly men with guns pointing at him. Till now, they had never run into such a situation.

"So, there's more of you that live up here?" the major asked. "I thought it was just you six.

"Well, you thought wrong," Rusty growled, then spit a yard of brown juice into the dirt beside the porch. He was trying to make a point, but the man didn't seem to care.

"I thought you were already turned around and heading back from where ya came," Rusty barked. "It's none of your business who does and who don't live up here. Maybe we be a hundred strong. So, you can mosey back down to that patrol of yours and ride back down the mountain. The local Indians will make short work of y'all up here. They know these woods like the backs of their hands."

The major smiled, grabbed a seat from a peg on the wall, and sat down, ignoring Rusty, whose face was so red it looked like it would burst.

"I didn't say I had anybody with me," the major replied.

"You sure are a pushy fella, ain't cha," Syracuse Sam said.

"Are ya gonna shoot me or not?" the major asked blandly. Now, he surprised the mountain men even more. What kind of soldier was this? "Well, spit it out. I need to know if I have to defend myself or not. If you're going to do it, please, at least wait until I've finished my coffee." He sipped loudly so Rusty could hear.

"I've seen people kicked in the head by a horse who

has more sense than you do, mister," Rusty said. "Are you dumb, or ya just bein' ornery?"

Still, the major ignored Rusty and sipped his coffee like he was sitting with six old friends. But he was the only one being friendly. You couldn't even call it friendly because there was an arrogance about the man they didn't expect. That, or he was plumb crazy.

"Of all the chicken-headed, swamp-water muskrats I've ever seen, you take the cake," Rusty spat as he sat down, wrapped his fingers around his hot tin cup, and stared at the officer ignoring him.

UNWANTED REUNION

IN THE DISTANCE, THE MOUNTAIN MEN HEARD THE SOFT sound of horses' hooves crunching fresh, ice-covered snow. Vapor rose from the animals' mouths and noses. Two mules packed high with pelts sauntered behind the riders as they rode into view. Levi Johnson led and had his rifle across his lap. He, too, had smelled the fancy soap. It reminded him of something, but he couldn't put his finger on it. The odor was familiar, but he didn't connect it with danger. He still hadn't noticed the soldier sitting at the table with his friends. The sun was low on the horizon, casting long shadows, partially covering the men on the porch.

Johnson and Forrester had been gone for ten days without a single sign of danger. The area they'd discovered with the large spring was so far off the beaten path that nobody knew it was there. Of course, massive tracts of the Rocky Mountains had never been seen by White men's eyes. Some parts were still unseen by Indian eyes too. The two young mountain men had had to forge a new path to arrive where they heard falling water. Levi was proud they had done so well on their first trip out for beaver out of many to come during the following winter months. He was having the time of his life, doing exactly what he had dreamed about all his youth.

In a narrow creek, he had set two new traps he had invented. They were for fish that lived in the streams. It was good to keep phosphorus in their diet along with lots of protein. On the first day, he'd caught a bonanza of fish. They hung frozen on stringers across the back of Levi's mule, Dot. As the temperatures dropped, they could keep them in the storage shed where it would be zero or below for most of the winter. Their lifestyle gobbled up energy like dogs to biscuits. Especially the two young men. Of course, neither were boys.

They were in their mid-twenties. Will was slightly older. For the wilderness, it wasn't young by any measure, but most men that age didn't have enough experience to survive in the Rockies. Johnson was one of those few who had no trouble thriving and was even becoming wise in his knowledge of the out-of-doors and the White man's relationships with Indians.

Will rode behind Levi. He, too, wore a bearskin coat with it pulled high to his ears. His ears were what suffered from the cold, despite wading in waters of creeks and streams, drenched from the waist down. They were blood red and stung from the sudden cold. He was afraid to touch them, fearing they break off—it was Forrester's weak point. He had to remember to make a raccoon skin cap first thing upon their return. He had used his scarf for this trip, and it quickly slipped from his ears. He planned to make a new cap in the next few days.

If not, his ears would become frostbit during the

depths of winter—if they didn't fall off first. They had every type of pelt known in the Rocky Mountains. He would choose some soft rabbit fur to line the inside. Since Levi came from the woods in southwestern Indiana, he was no stranger to heavy snow and freezing weather. As a boy, it was the bread and butter of every day during the winter. But it rarely stopped him from hunting. It was even easier because the prints were so visible in the snow.

He remembered many nights running behind Blue and Toby, the family dogs. They would race through the dark on the trail of a raccoon. It was tough going, and you had to be quick, but the furs made great caps—especially if he lined it with rabbit. Levi brushed the snow from his head with his hand.

"I got hit by the little drifts on the overhead branches." Levi smiled. He rode a big horse, and he towered over the animal. "Whatcha think about that bunch of pelts, Rusty?"

"Where did ya find 'em?" Rusty replied. "That's a passel of furs."

"We found an undiscovered valley," Levi said. He was beginning to get excited. It was a significant find. "We cut a trail there. We heard the water running out of a crack in a rock and making a crystal pool. It's maybe fifty meters wide, twice as long, and plenty deep. It's high up, so several streams overspill into creeks down the mountain. I reckon it's like that all year around."

Will couldn't think of anything except siding up to the fire inside the cabin where he could thaw out his ears. Both men wore heavy beards and buckskin clothing. They looked like they had been born in the Rocky Mountains.

"We'll tend to the horses, store the pelts and then get some hot coffee in us," Levi Beaver Johnson said. "I hope that kettle's full when we get back. Whose turn is it today? We'd have been here last night if it weren't for the snow."

"It's me," Angus grumbled. "Go on now, young fellas, and when ya get back, I'll have some hot biscuits to go with the coffee."

Like all the men, Angus had taken a special shine to Levi. He was born to live this way of life. The young man was the best shot they had ever seen, although Rusty still wouldn't admit it. He liked to make sure they were well-fed. As it was, they ate twice as much as the others who were older men.

"So, those two fellas are mountain men too?" the major asked.

Surprised, the men looked at him like they hadn't expected him to be there. Like they had believed he had already left. Unfriendly eyes bored into the stranger, but he didn't seem to notice or care. He broke out a pouch of tobacco and made a hand-built, popped it in his mouth, and lit up.

By the time the two got back, steam floated in the air from the iron frying pan skillet full of hot biscuits. The gallon pot of coffee was full. Bubbles popped from the spout. The major had stepped out to water his horse. It used its hooves to brush away the snow to get at the green grass below.

The horse, like its master, ignored everybody. Both man and beast had a confidence that bordered on arrogance. He hadn't said anything out of order but still refused to leave. The mountain men exchanged looks, and they all thought the same. It looked like they were going to have to remove the fancy pants major physically. If he wanted, Levi could do it alone.

Beaver Johnson burned his fingers on the pan, picking up a biscuit. He popped it into his mouth as he waved his hand before his face trying to cool it down. It burned his mouth and all the way down to his stomach. It left a warm glow inside. He sipped at piping hot coffee.

"Wait till they cool some before ya burn your tongue off." Angus cackled. "You look to be half starved, Levi. Come on, Will, there's two for you too."

Will could hear the squeak of leather boots at his back. He breathed in, and a subtle tremor racked his body from the top of his head to the ground. He was so rattled that the earth beneath his feet felt as if it was gone.

"Are there more of you mountain men here or is this the last of your bunch?" the major asked.

Rusty snapped a look over his shoulder and shot daggers at the soldier. "Are you still around? Why don't you just skedaddle on out of here? There ain't a thing here for the likes of you. Do you have difficulties understanding the words *no* and *go*?"

The major sipped at his coffee as he casually cocked his head, leaned against the building, and hung his boot on a chair. If he heard what Rusty Steel had said, it wasn't apparent. He stared at the snow-covered yard like he was thinking about someplace else.

Captain Will Forrester was shaken to his very core. His stomach clawed its way to his throat, and he swallowed it back as sweat broke out on his face. He took a deep breath before he turned, and he smelled it too. The same soap he had used when he came to the frontier forts. It was store-bought back from the big cities in the East. On the inside, he felt like a grasshopper on loco weed, although he had learned how to hide his feelings early in life. But this was more like an earth-quake for him, shocking his core and threatening his sanity.

"Well, I best be on my way," the major said. "I can see what I'm lookin' for ain't here."

He knew the man's voice like he knew his own. *Could it be?* Will asked himself. Forrester slowly turned and looked at the officer. He was staring at his horse.

Will tried to talk, but the words didn't come out. His mouth opened and closed like a beached fish. Levi was the only one to notice. He sniffed the air, looked into Will's eyes, then his locked with the major.

"Why, you two look like kin," Levi Johnson whis-pered. Will was still too tongue-tied to speak, but the comment got the major's attention.

He turned, his brow furrowed as his eyes narrowed, and he looked closer at the young mountain man. He noticed his folded right sleeve where he was missing an arm. He hesitated momentarily, like his mind was having difficulty wrapping itself around who the man standing in front of him might be.

Finally, Forrester managed to grin through his beard at his uncle—his father's brother. He immediately recognized Will's eyes. They were the same baby blue eyes he saw as a kid. He smiled at his nephew for the mountain men's sake, but the smile didn't reach his eyes. They said something else totally different. Anger boiled just below the surface. Nobody spoke for the longest time. The major held his tongue, so the words in his mind didn't walk out his mouth all on their own. He realized that a wrong word now could cost him his life.

Levi looked at his best friend and asked, "Ain't cha gonna introduce us to your uncle? Why is everybody actin' so strange?"

Now the mountain men knew why the soldier didn't want to talk. They didn't think he was there because he missed his young nephew either. Otherwise, he would have mentioned it right off. He was hiding something, and they wanted to know what it was. They weren't going to let anything happen to the two new members. They were now part of their clan, and it was all for one and one for all.

"Maybe you better ask Uncle Warren, er, I mean, Major Forrester of the Seventh Cavalry," Will sheepishly replied.

The major remained leaning on the wall as he drew on his cigarette and stared at his kin. His eyes were questioning, but despite the time passed since they last saw each other, they weren't friendly, and the major sure didn't act like a dear uncle and close family.

"What happened to your arm, William?" Major Forrester asked. "Was that why you ran off and abandoned your post, young man?"

Now his voice was all military, and his face stern. Levi got the feeling he wasn't there for a friendly visit.

Will Forrester had been browbeaten all his life by his military family. From his grandfather down, nearly all the men had been Army. Uncle Warren was no exception. But Will wasn't the same man he was the last time the major had seen him. That man was buried with the arm he lost.

Will looked at his uncle with a tiny smile on the edge of his lips and asked, "What arm?"

From the day Will decided to buck up to the loss, put it in his past, and now he was twice the man he was before he lost it. Now he refused to recognize the loss.

The major nodded and chuckled. Now, the humor hit his eyes, but still, they were guarded.

"I'd say we've got some talking to do, Captain Forrester," Warren said it like it was an order and not a request.

Will cleared his throat, trying to ease some of the tension out of his words.

"William Forrester. That's my name, even though my friends call me Will. I'm not that captain back at Fort Leavenworth anymore. He's buried somewhere around here in a grave about that long." He showed the length of his empty sleeve. "I'm a mountain man now and will never return to the Army. Not after what I've seen being done to the Indians."

"Do you realize what you're saying, William?" Warren asked. "If your grandfather heard you now, he'd turn over in his grave."

PUZZLED MINDS

"NOW, HOLD ON A DAD-GUMMED MINUTE," RUSTY SPAT. "Who gave you the right to talk? This is my house, my porch, and my friends you're pushin' around and trespassing on, and I won't tolerate it."

Steel's fingers drummed on a pistol grip in his belt like he was thinking about shooting the sassy officer. His eyes narrowed like he was ready to blow his stack. Rusty's temper was famous over the mountains. During normal times, he was cool-headed, although usually grumpy. But when provoked or threatened, he turned into a rattler and could strike at any moment.

Angus had lived with him in the same cabin for years and was the first to see the signs. If Rusty was too riled up, he was prone to violence. Of course, it was always dosed out in fair measures and only to those who deserved it, like the major. Steel stared at him like he wanted to put a bullet in him.

This was something his friends were aware of. Angus snuck around the back of Rusty, and as soon as he saw he was going to make his move, he lassoed him like he was cattle. He loop-trapped his arms by his sides. Then Angus yanked the rope and pulled him backward, leaving him off balance. Rusty fell off the porch and landed on his butt in the fresh snow. When angered, the aging mountain man seemed to have blinders on and could only see red and straight ahead.

He shook his head as though to clear it of cobwebs. Then he shot an angry look over his shoulder at Angus, but he held his tongue because he knew he was only doing it for his own good. It wouldn't be the first nosey stranger to stop by and nearly get shot.

"Rusty! It's me, Angus. Stop it right now before ya shoot somebody. I ain't gonna let ya go until ya calm down and promise me you won't hurt the major."

This behavior caught both Levi and Will by surprise. They'd never seen Rusty explode like this, and he did it to protect them. Sam, Pete, Dennis, and Bob had become used to it over the years. They each had been the ones to rope him at one time or another. When he was really mad, they had to tie the rope off a saddle horn and stop him with a horse as he tugged forward as stubbornly as a mule. He reacted to things without thinking of the consequences when he got that angry. They weren't doing it just to save the odd stranger but to keep their friend out of trouble with the law.

"Iffin I was you, mister, I'd get out of here," Dennis said, smiling. He found it all amusing. "The longer you stay, the less chance you'll have of leavin'."

"Everybody's got to die sometime," Warren replied with a deadpan voice. When they looked into his eyes, he suddenly appeared tired and defeated.

Even though the major was hell-bent on convincing Will to go back East, it was apparent he had doubts about his own part in the massacre of masses of Indians. He was even more moved by the loss of so many of his men. He didn't have one man he considered a friend to survive the battles on the plains. Those, along with the patrol wiped out by Buffalo Hump in Texas, were nearly more than his mind could bear. He had a deep hate for the Indians he had been fighting for longer than he could remember.

"Have a seat before ya fall down, Major," Angus said. "Don't pay Rusty no mind. He's threatened to kill most of us here at one time or another."

Yet another fact that made Levi and Will's eyes spread and their chins drop to their chests. They had seen how onery Rusty was, but they had always seen him as wise and not the type to fly off the handle and shoot a soldier for nothing more than entering the compound uninvited. They didn't realize he acted this way because the Army officer talked about Levi and Will. All six mountain men were as protective of them as a grizzly bear mama to her cubs, even if the major was his uncle.

"When he was a young fella, he was hell on wheels." Dennis laughed. Angus helped him remove the rope. "Even at his age, he still jumps off the rails once in a while. Iffin you just keep an eye on 'im and don't turn your back, you should be all right." Dennis continued to snicker. "You may just ride out of here alive."

Angus smiled and said, "Stop leaning on the wall like ya was a broom and have a seat. There's more hot coffee iffin ya want."

The look on Will Forrester's face was more defiant than ever. He had always intended to stand up to his family at some point in the future, but rather than being able to pick the time, it had come to him. As far as he was concerned, he hadn't done anything wrong and had made the only right choice for himself. Of course, it was still early to see if he had all he needed to survive in the mountains like the original inhabitants of the compound. One thing he was sure of—he wasn't going back to Fort Leavenworth with his uncle.

Forrester knew Levi already had the stuff it took to be a mountain man. He was determined to learn what he needed to, despite losing his arm. It had given him a renewed inspiration and challenge in life, and he hadn't looked back since they buried it, not until today. Now, he could no longer ignore it. He had to face his recent past as not only a family member but to an officer of the United States Army.

Will should have known somebody in his family would be so upset with his actions that they would try to find him and drag him back. But he wasn't the same man he was back then. Now, nobody was going to drag him anywhere he didn't want to go. Of course, he knew his family would never change. For them, the only honorable position for a Forrester was in one of the American armed forces.

And when one of their family became a soldier, he was also expected to serve in combat. That was why there were so many pictures of dead male members of his family on photographs on the wall. They honored the dead like they were trophies. If he died, it would be another legacy for his father—something he didn't plan on doing, no matter who thought what.

"No matter what you say, I'm not going back with you, Warren," Will said, determined. He locked eyes with his uncle. "I won't let anybody bring you harm here either. You are my family, after all. You're welcome to stay for a day or two like any other friend of ours would if they came to visit. After that, I'm afraid you'll have to leave like everybody else. We came here to live to escape civilization and all it represented. I know, in a way, I came here to escape the Army too, but more than that, to escape the faces of the men I sent to their deaths. But that was then, and now is now. I've changed a lot since then. That's probably why Rusty here hasn't thrown me out." He smiled, and it reached his eyes.

There was a new kindness there. Every day, it seemed to the two young men they were taught some new lesson about the wilderness, themselves, or life.

"You get me so mad I could smoke a pickle," Rusty growled, "but I reckon I can't turn ya away, though, iffin your kin to one of *us*." He emphasized that they were like family, maybe more so than his uncle.

Steel wanted to make it clear that Levi and Will were each one of them, and if he tried to take one away, it would mean he would have to deal with all eight. They felt more like Levi and Will's family than his uncle, who was always somewhere fighting some battles while his nephew was growing up. It was the same with his father. They both lived for the Army, and their family always came second. Of course, America needed men like them for the services to work, but sometimes the priorities got mixed up with politics, and now, for the Army, the Indians had to go.

Warren sat and stared at Rusty for a minute—he looked defeated and angry simultaneously. Then he turned his eyes on Will.

"I hardly recognized you, William," the major huffed. "You've changed so much. Your mother and father would be shocked, to say the least. We never expected you to do anything but follow in our footsteps, but I'm afraid you've let us down. You're putting me on the spot now, boy. Be careful of what you say next. If you shame us, we'll disown you."

"I'm no longer a boy, Warren," Will replied. "I'm a grown man who killed too many men—just like you. So don't call me that—don't call me boy. Nobody asked you to come here, so you put yourself on the spot, not me. Not everybody is cut out for West Point and a military career. If it weren't for my father and family like you, I would have chosen something else to do with my life, but none of you ever let me. You never even asked."

Ex-Captain Forrester of the United States Army looked hard at his uncle. It was like he was seeing him for the first time. He'd never looked at him like any other man before. He had looked up to his uncle, but now he saw the real Major Warren Forrester. He was little more than a facade of his own lies.

"My passion was geography—you know that. It was what made me jump at the chance to study mapmaking when I went to West Point. I thought I had found my true calling, but I was mistaken. Comanche decimated my expedition to map the way westward, and you ask me why I quit? Maybe you should take a look at yourself for a change. Was it your choice to become who you are? Maybe you should have a good look in the mirror, because you've changed even more than me from the last time I saw you. You're a shell of the man I knew as a boy, and you ask me why I don't want to return?"

"Don't trust 'im, Will," Angus whispered in Will's ear. "He's only worried about himself. He doesn't want your decision to change your life for the better. He just don't want you to blemish the family name. I doubt he has an ounce of love left in that scarred-up heart of his."

The major gave Angus a dirty look. Warren didn't like the way he was being treated. He wasn't used to hearing the word *no*. If the truth was known, he didn't like mountain men either. He saw them as nearly half-breeds, which he detested, and his eyes didn't hide his disdain for Angus or Rusty.

"I didn't come here to talk about me. I came here to talk some sense into that thick head of yours. Are you sure about what you're doing?" Warren asked. "Your grades were exemplary. We all expected great things from you. Are you going to throw all that away for this? To live almost like the heathens that murder innocent settlers and kidnap women and children?"

"I know what you came here for, but nobody asked me what I wanted to do," Will replied. "You and dad had my life all figured out without consulting me on a darned thing."

"That's because young men always make mistakes, and we were steering you in the right direction," Warren said, but it didn't sound like even he believed it but was too bullheaded to allow the thought to linger.

"And how'd that work out for you, Major?" Rusty asked. "I doubt I've ever met a man with so much baggage and weight on his shoulders as you. It shows in your face, your eyes, and even how you move. You walk like you dread each next step you take. I reckon you look like a man who's been considerin' some dark things, ain't cha now?"

Rusty knew Will had struck a nerve from how Warren glared at him. He had seen men like him. Heck, he was similar when he first ran off to the mountains.

He wondered how strong the major's will was to remain what and who he was. His nephew seemed to shun it quickly enough. When you live with the Indians, you see everything differently. After some time living so close to the Crow, Rusty believed a man couldn't help but respect them for their noble ways.

That and their battle to keep what was theirs for the last ten thousand years. He knew he and the Army would never see things the same way, just like he knew how things would ultimately work out for the Indian Nations. They were bedeviled because of the Major Foresters out there. They were doomed by Washington as soon as they began to give away Indian land like it was theirs to give.

Rusty's wisdom ran deeper than most thought. He saw the big picture better than the other mountain men. He knew what was coming even though everyone living a life like theirs denied it. He hoped to teach these two young men his knowledge of the wilderness because he didn't believe there would be another generation of mountain men. With the closing in of civilization, they were a dying breed.

He was lucky enough to have two strong men willing to take on the challenge just like he, Dennis, and Angus did for all these years. The men who lived in the Rocky Mountains looked at the range of peaks like they were their mothers—scolding them when they were careless and gifting them with incredible beauty with every sunrise. When they were careful and respected all those who lived around them, whether they be men or beasts, the wilderness was kind in turn. Betray that trust and the punishment would come fast and furious.

BUFFALO HUMP

THE MAJOR SAT AND STARED INTO HIS COFFEE AGAIN AS HE swirled the black liquid around and around. He felt like he was a dog chasing its own tail. If he was truthful, he'd never looked in the mirror to see the changes he might have experienced. He shaved most days, but that wasn't the same thing. He knew he was unhappy. On one hand, he was proud of what he was doing for his country. On the other, he felt a nagging suspicion that his actions might block his way past the pearly gates. He had always felt following orders couldn't be a sin. Now that he looked back, he wasn't so sure anymore.

"I've never talked about it before," Warren Forrester whispered. "Those of us who were there get nervous when we speak of those times. We can't look each other in the eye. For the people who weren't there, we don't really know how to explain it. At least not to anybody I know."

"You have now." Rusty grinned. "There ain't a man here who ain't fought for their lives against the

Comanche, and I'd say your nephew more than us all. At least he and Levi."

"There ain't nothin' more terrifyin' than a Comanche war cry," Dennis said with a faraway look. "I've been here the longest, and everybody is scared of 'em—even the other Indians. They rarely make it to the mountains, but we saw our share in Kansas, didn't we, boys? Sometimes we have the misfortune to make unwise decisions, and we found ourselves in Kansas this summer. We would have never returned alive if it weren't for these two young men. You can call Will what cha want, but I won't have ya callin' him a coward or a quitter, because he ain't either."

The major nodded. He was beginning to understand, at least a little. They were right; he was torn apart and nearly used up. He also held many dark secrets about himself and his future plans.

"It was that rascal Buffalo Hump we chased," Major Warren Forrester said slowly, like he was picking his words. "Actually, lots of the time, he was chasing us."

"When did all this happen?" Sam asked. "I ain't heard a word."

"You ain't heard a word because we're up here in the mountains, Syracuse," Rusty said. "Sometimes you're as dumb as two marbles in a tin can. Now let the man talk. It'll do 'im good to get it off his chest."

"August sixth, Buffalo Hump organized five hundred warriors from several tribes. They rode from their stronghold and into Central Texas, and the war party split up. Part of them attacked Victoria. They rode right through the center of the city. The Texas Rangers, the Texan militia, and our patrol were tracking them, but the war party was massive. Nobody had ever seen anything like it, so we didn't dare attack."

"I've seen hundreds of Indians but with women and children," Pete said in nearly a whisper. "I can't imagine what it'd be like to run into five hundred Comanche with painted faces and in a war party."

"We watched it from afar with the Texas Rangers. I don't think the Texans wanted us there, but they didn't have the authority to tell Army soldiers to leave, and my orders were to find hostiles and stop them. Buffalo Hump and a couple hundred warriors rode right into the middle of the town and killed a dozen citizens. Then the hostiles looted the stores until, finally, the locals began to return rifle fire from the cover of their homes and businesses.

"We worked on picking them off with rifles at a safe distance. We were a few hands-full of men compared to them and three hundred more outside of town. Lucky for us, eventually they came under too much fire, and the Comanche retreated and rejoined the main war party. That night, we saw that they camped on Spring Creek. The next day, they rode to Placido Creek and made camp again. It was only twelve miles from town. As far as we could tell, they were closing in to attack the city, which was something unheard of. Sure, they'd picked off isolated settlers and stolen cattle, but this time they headed for civilization and struck at its heart.

"They surrounded Linnville, and the citizens' only refuge was on the water," Warren continued. "They escaped to a schooner and dozens of small boats. They bobbed in the water of the bay and watched as the Comanche looted and stole everything of value they had. Then they burned the port town to the ground.

Lucky for the residents, they had the water for escape. The Comanche weren't prepared to pursue them over water—they are Plains Indians. They say the fire that night was engraved in the minds of all that saw it. The town is in ashes, and I doubt it'll ever be rebuilt again. That was just two months ago."

"Gosh, I never heard nothin' like it," Angus said in a hushed voice. Nobody wanted to see five hundred Comanche in the same place.

"From there, the war party just kept growing. After Victoria, they were nearing six hundred braves, but by the time they made it to Linnville and the port, they were a thousand warriors strong. They attacked the second biggest port in Texas."

The major stopped and made a hand-built cigarette. Nobody said a word. They were all mesmerized by the story, which was undoubtedly true. These things only happened a few weeks ago. It wasn't another rumor that ran through the Indian gossip like poop through a goose. Angus took a swig from the jug sitting in the center of the table to calm his nerves. The story had all the mountain men anxious.

Cicadas chattered in the distance, but not another sound was heard. A breeze made the trees sway, and the smell of pine floated on puffs of air. The sun stood overhead as it warmed the earth, but not enough to melt the snow. The temperatures were dropping in the Rockies as winter neared.

"When did you run into them?" Will asked. "The Comanche, I mean."

The younger Forrester was as absorbed as them all. For a moment, he forgot why his uncle was there. Especially after his battle with the Comanche while traveling across Kansas, he knew what Warren went through. They were all scared to death when face-to-face with Comanche warriors. He couldn't imagine a thousand of them. That would be enough to stop a man's heart. Anybody that said differently was a liar, a fool, or maybe both. Everybody there had lost somebody to these fiercely dreaded warrior braves. The men all sat on the edges of their seats. The air was tense. Warren struck a match and lit his cigarette. The smell of sulfur filled the air.

"We had a small detachment of fourteen men, and we attached to the militia and Rangers," Warren said. "The fort commander thought we were enough to fend them off and kill them all if necessary. If not, they wanted us to take the remaining Comanche to a reservation. We had no idea what we were about to run into."

"What was a major doin' runnin' around the country chasin' Indians? I thought that was for captains and down," Rusty said.

"I volunteered," Warren replied. "I wanted to do my part to do my duty to eliminate the hostile Indians." He almost felt guilty but didn't know why.

"I doubt a Comanche goes to any reservations." Portland Pete chuckled. His black hair stuck out from under his fur cap, and his cheeks always seemed drawn in, even though he ate everybody out of house and home. He was missing several teeth.

"We had the first major clash on Plum Creek," Warren said. "That's when we ran into Buffalo Hump. They were slowed down by the mules they stole to carry everything they looted back to their camp all the way across Texas. That's the only reason we could keep up with them. From there, it was a running battle. Sometimes we were after them and sometimes they were after us. We were terribly outnumbered. Finally, the Comanche gave up the silver bullion and everything else they stole but a small herd of horses, but I reckon Buffalo Hump was just trying to make a point anyway. As soon as the militia and the few Rangers left got sight of the silver, then and there they abandoned the fight, divided the loot, and went home."

"And what did you do, Uncle Warren?" Will asked.

All their eyes were spread wide. He told it with so much feeling they felt like they were there. This was the first time he'd ever talked about one of his battles. He was reliving it like he was there again. They could see him struggle. It was in his face and eyes.

"They stole over three thousand horses and mules," the major said like he was in a trance. "We continued the chase, but they were on the run by then. I believe had they turned on us, we would have all undoubtedly died. As it was, I lost ten of fourteen men, and even the survivors were wounded. The Rangers suffered light casualties like the militia because they went home. They had the money, half of the horses, and the Indians on the run and believed they had done their job. I guess we were the only ones to try to chase them across Texas. We only made it halfway, then my sergeant, our corporal, two privates, and I returned to San Antonio. My orders cost me my men, but that's how the Army is. Who was to know those wicked heathens would be able to gather a thousand braves at one time."

"Then why in the world did ya go if you knew you couldn't win?" Angus asked. "Just because some fool back in Washington who's never seen a Comanche tells ya to? It was probably the same bunch of fools that sent

Will on the excursion across the Rocky Mountains to find sites for forts. People tellin' ya who to kill and where to go when they've never been there nor have they seen an Indian other than in the newspapers or nickel novels."

"They were my orders, Mr. Angus," Warren said. "I never disobey orders. And these didn't come from Washington. They came from my commanding officer, General Stone. He wanted his men to be part of the capture of Buffalo Hump." He stared hard at his nephew.

Warren Forrester was torn between right and wrong and didn't know how to proceed. *Did I make all the wrong decisions, too?* he asked himself. For a second, the fleeting question went through his head. He tried to shove it back into the dark recesses of his mind, but it didn't want to go.

Rusty stared at the green-eyed major and asked, "And how's that workin' out for ya? I mean, following all of them orders and all. I bet some of those orders don't sit quite right with ya now, do they? Ain't I right? Crow's hard to swallow when it's cold. So, they sent ya here to get the boy, did they?"

The major stared into his cup and thought about his life and what he was doing.

"No, they didn't send me here to bring Captain William Forrester back to Fort Leavenworth. They were going to send someone else. So, I volunteered to hunt my nephew down. I came because I felt it was my responsibility."

Everybody heard Will and Levi gasp. Johnson pushed his chair back and stood as he towered over the officer. His hands were bunched into massive fists.

"Will's my best friend, so you'll be takin' him back over my dead body, Mister," Levi threatened and stared hard at the soldier. "I'm not afraid of you. You're just another man up here. Mother Nature gives the orders around here—her and God. There ain't no courts of law or barracks up here. All ya got is what cha see."

Just like Johnson, all the men spouted hackles and grew angry and grumbled. Eight sets of eyes stared at the lone officer. He stared back like he was asking them to try to stop him. That was when Warren realized: he couldn't say no. He couldn't walk away any more than he could stop breathing. He had to stand up to them even if they killed him because his orders told him to. Why he did it, he wasn't really even sure. It was how he was trained to respond. It was his job. It was his duty.

"You sure do have a set of stones on you, Mister," Rusty spat. "But nobody is takin' either of our boys from us. We might not be blood like you, but we're more of a family to him than you've ever been."

"That may be, but that doesn't change my orders," Warren said. "Apparently, we're stuck at an impasse."

"And exactly where are those orders, if I may be so bold to ask?" Will said.

Young Forrester wasn't afraid of his uncle like he had been when he was young. As a lifer in the Army, his uncle was seldom around and didn't have a family, and he picked now to look up his own flesh and blood. He stood there before him with an empty sleeve.

"So, what made ya run off and leave your command, Will?" Warren asked. "And that question is coming from me. The brass doesn't care why you did what you did. It's still desertion to them."

His voice was softer, but his face was hard, like it was chiseled in stone. His eyes were distant, like he was looking somewhere else far away. His body was only going through the motions as though it was on automatic pilot.

"You, his own flesh and blood, are ready to take him back to Kansas to be court-martialed and sent to prison?" Angus spat. "Is that what folks do to their families back in Washington? I'm afraid we treat our kin a mite better here."

"It will go better for him if I can say he gave himself up," Warren said. "But he must pay for what he did just like any other Army officer."

"I lost more than half of my command and the most important scientist," Will replied. "I wasn't sent out to fight Indians. We were going to map the route to build more frontier forts to protect the settlers. The geologist would take samples, and I would chart the maps as I learned in West Point."

"Don't you dare mention West Point to me," Warren huffed, suddenly angry—he was about to lose his cool. "I never want to hear those words come from your mouth again. Do you understand me, boy?"

"I don't see where you're in a position to tell anybody what to do or not do," Levi growled. Will had been like a brother to him, and he knew he had the stuff to make it as a mountain man. He'd also witnessed his failure as a soldier. "Some men weren't meant to be soldiers, despite their family's opinion. When I met Will, he was a soldier, and to be honest, I didn't like him much, nor did his men. Then, after what we went through together and how we changed, I thought he might just have a chance to live a life of kings. He also went through his tough times, but in the end, he became a better man and my best friend."

"Do you call this living like kings?" Warren asked, shocked. "You're no more than a handful of hermits living like heathens."

"Oh, but that's where you're wrong, Uncle Warren," Will said. "There is beauty here worth more than any pot of gold at the end of a rainbow. Spend a few days with us and let us show you why we want to live here and nowhere else."

"And what would you have me tell your father if I returned without you?" Major Forrester asked. "You will be more of a disgrace in his eyes if you don't come home with me."

"He was the one who sent me to military school," Will said. "Nobody ever asked me if I wanted to go. He enrolled me into West Point without my consent too. It was like it was meant to be. It's not that I was a coward, either. This I have proved over and over in front of these men here. I decided I didn't want my father deciding my life for me. Just like your and dad's father did to you. I heard the stories about granddad. You're more like him than you are like your brother. At least my father didn't come and track me down like some sort of outlaw."

CROW CAMP

"WHY DON'T WE SHOW THE MAJOR WHAT INDIANS ARE really like?" Levi asked. He felt he had to find a way to work things out with Will and his uncle. He knew what would happen if he tried to force or arrest him to return home and on to some federal prison for years, if not life. How could a family member wish such a thing on his own kind? "I bet the only ones you've seen are the ones you were shootin' at. I bet if you met them in a peaceful situation, you'd see things different."

"Now you're talking nonsense," the major replied. "I'm an Indian fighter. They'll know what I am as soon as they see me, and I'll know who the warriors are too. There'll be no love lost between us."

"Maybe it wasn't for as long as you, but Will did his fair share of fighting Indians, too," Levi said. "At first, he didn't side up to the idea much either. He was my boss, and I was workin' as an Army scout. Yeah, I've worked for the Army too. But with time, your nephew grew to love our way of life just like I do. Sometimes we don't

54ASH LINGAM

give things a chance, and never know what might have been."

"I told you that boy would become wiser than you, Rusty." Angus laughed. "Now he's preachin' to us and all."

"Whatcha say, Major?" Levi asked. "It can't hurt cha none. If you're willin' to take on the whole bunch of us, why not take on a tribe of a hundred warriors? If you're lookin' for an enemy, I can introduce ya to ten dozen."

Now that the anger fit had passed, Warren caught a fit of laughter just at the thought of Levi's proposal. It was preposterous. He had to admit, in some ways, his orders were silly and had no point either, but he left the bigger picture to his superiors to figure out. Despite his high rank, he was a boots-on-the-ground type of officer. He also found that going into an Indian camp as anything but an enemy was hilarious.

His body began to convulse with laughter, and his eyes swelled with tears. They streamed down his face as a long spool of saliva hung from his mouth and dangled in the breeze. But the laugh sounded nervous and almost crazy. Will looked at his uncle with concern, despite his orders and intentions.

Suddenly, Warren felt like he didn't weigh more than a feather. He took three deep breaths and smiled. His burdens seemed to have lifted, at least for a while. After a few minutes, he regained his composure, and although embarrassed, he did feel better, having gotten some of what he had done and seen off his chest.

The following day, everybody went with Levi, Will, and the major to the Crow camp. Of course, Rusty Steel always jumped at the chance to visit his old friend Chief Hachta. Especially since he hadn't had a chance to see him since he had gone from war chief to the tribe's chief. Now, he ruled over the entire camp. He knew Will hoped his uncle would understand that all Indians weren't the same as those that attacked his men and burned towns and killed people across the state of Texas.

Not all tribes were as hostile and unforgiving as the Comanche. Young Forrester knew they were just getting revenge for the theft of their land and the blatant killing of their people by White men. They were doing the same thing they themselves would do if the tables were turned. This appeared to be what nobody but a few saw. The mountain men were among that few. They saw both sides of the story and realizing that there was no solution in sight weighed heavy on their minds.

Usually, somebody stayed behind in the compound. But the camp was only a half-day's ride, and nobody wanted to miss whatever happened to the Indian fighter when he met peaceful Indians for the first time. That, and to ensure he didn't do something they all would regret. He had been killing Indians for some time and had experienced some of the worst engagements the Army had ever had with the native tribes. His scars ran wide and deep, and they were visible as soon as he opened his mouth. It showed on his scared face and in the thousand-yard stare in his eyes.

They left expecting to return before the end of the day. Will and Levi stabled the mules, and the mountain men locked their cabins up tight. They rode out right as the first light from the sun marked a new day. As they climbed higher into the mountains, long shadows made them appear to be eighteen riders.

"What should I say to the Indians?" Warren asked

his nephew. They rode spur to spur. "I don't speak, Crow."

"Don't worry about what to say," Will said. "I'm more worried you'll say too much."

"I reckon the less he talks, the better for everybody," Levi said as he shot a glance over his shoulder. "Chief Hachta speaks pretty good English. He said he learned from the early missionaries. He speaks Spanish too. Once, I heard him tell Rusty if you want to keep your enemies close, you had to understand what they said. I reckon today we'll be putting that to the test."

"Remember, he'll understand most everything you say, so if you go all sassy, he'll be offended, and even I won't be able to save ya," Rusty warned. "Just mind your manners, and don't kill anybody, and we'll be all right."

The men's and horses' breaths were seen as they climbed higher, and temperatures continued to drop. They all wore buffalo robes. Will couldn't sleep a wink the previous night, so he spent the evening making a warm hat. The raccoon's tail hung down his back, and the rabbit fur covered his ears enough to keep them warm. His nose was as red as a tomato, but he was warm inside his thick bearskin robe. Today, they wouldn't be wading in freezing creeks and streams. They were on a dangerous adventure. The young mountain man was both excited and scared.

Everybody, including Warren, wondered how things would go when they arrived in a large Crow camp with an Indian killer. He imagined they were all fools, and the Indians would attack them. His pistols were loaded with fresh powder, and all four were in his belt. His saber hung from his right side. This was how William had looked when he departed for the western frontier.

To his uncle, he now looked like a bum—a scavenger that preyed on the leftovers of the Indians. If he had a week in this mountain, he would rid it of every warrior above fourteen years of age. If they were old enough to carry a bow, they were old enough to die.

Of course, Warren knew he might die that very day in the Crow Indian camp. He almost wished it to be. What better way to go out than taking the chief, war chief, and as many medicine men as he could with him in a blaze of glory? It would leave the camp in chaos. If he did survive and could escape, he would return with a few patrols, and they would eliminate the warriors, round up the women and children for the reservations, and burn the village.

Then he would hogtie William if he had to and drag his butt back to face the consequences. Even if he was a Forrester, he wasn't above the Army's rules and laws. He wondered why the mountain men thought it was a good idea for him to go. At this point, he didn't resist but let destiny lead them all to wherever they were going. He knew he might be going to hell.

Nine horses climbed the narrow, snow-covered trail. Now they rode in a single file. The trail was cut from a cliff with a hundred-yard drop to the bottom. Until they passed, they saw no footprints, so nobody had been on this trail since the day before, at least. Despite their friendship with the Crow Indians, Rusty Steel kept his eyes sharp, looking for some sign of danger in the distance. He knew it was a dodgy move taking an Indian fighter into Hachta's camp, but when Levi proposed it, he thought it was a grand idea. Now he wasn't so sure about his decision. Maybe he should have said no, but now it was too late. Hindsight was a stickler at times.

As they rode through the forest, morning rays of light slanted through the trees like rain. Birds chattered and fluttered from branch to branch, and there was no sign of another human being. Grasshoppers jumped onto the riders only to launch themselves into flight again and land on a plant. But even as they climbed, word of their pending arrival had already been relayed.

Rusty looked into the sky and saw the smoke. He shook his head and said, "They already know we're coming. They'll be waiting for us. I was kind of hopin' we'd catch 'em by surprise."

"How could the Crow know we're riding for their camp when we only left three hours ago," Warren grumbled doubtfully. "Not even an Indian can ride that fast."

"Look up at the sky, fool," Rusty spat. "That there's smoke signals. They can send a message for miles in a few minutes. You seem to have the notion that the Indians ain't very clever. Boy, oh, boy, do you have a surprise in store for you."

The rest of the morning they rode in silence. The sign of smoke signals had suddenly reminded everyone that nothing happened in these mountains without the local natives knowing. They probably knew the moment the major entered the Rockies from the valley below. As the new chief, they weren't quite sure how Hachta would take to an Indian fighter roaming around their mountains spying on where they lived.

CROW CHIEF HACHTA

HACHTA SAT ON A BRIGHTLY COLORED BLANKET BEFORE A roaring fire. Heat radiated off the flames and orange coals. You could see he was shirtless beneath his heavy buffalo hide robe. He wore the chief's headdress just like Chief Chato had before him. It was dangerous being an Indian chief. You never knew when the tribe would become rife with discontent and decide they needed a new leader. For the time being, the new chief was as steady as a rock, just like he had been all his life. His friendship with Rusty went back to the time when the White man lived with the Crow Indians. He understood them in a way none of the other mountain men could.

He felt that Rusty Steel was his brother, and the other five he tolerated. Now, with the two new young mountain men in their compound, they had been the subject of talks and arguments among the tribe. As the White men came closer to their home, they knew the element of danger increased. Now, they were bringing a known Indian killer into their camp. The Plains Indians even had a name for this feared and ferocious fighter. They called him Angry Eyes because his eyes were always red and full of anger. He hated the Indians so much that he even killed boys before they could become warriors. He called those preventive tactics. He treated the elimination of the Indians like a White man's surgeon removed a leg.

Hachta believed that Rusty Steel didn't know who this demon of a man was. He wondered how he'd let him into his compound, let alone come to the home of his neighbors, the Crow. Angry Eyes was one of a half dozen killers the Army sent to lead their troops in decimating the Indian tribes. It appeared the major enjoyed what he did because he repeated his raids over and over again. One thing was for sure: the new Crow chief would never allow the wicked major to ride out of their camp. It would mean they would have to pull up stakes and leave immediately. There would be little time before he returned with his army of men.

The chief was the first to see the smoke signals from his scouts below near the mountain men's compound. He told his braves to prepare for their enemy's arrival; he painted his face with white, black, and red paint. White incisors were painted below the lips of a black face. A red line crossed his eyebrows and made a T down his nose. He painted thin red lines from his eyes, making them appear wildly terrifying. He and his warriors appeared every bit the demons the major made them out to be. They were almost as scary as the Comanche Indians.

All one hundred warriors stood behind the chief

waiting at the edge of the camp beside the trail. The party of White men would have to come this way. It was the only trail directly from their cabins to the Crow camp. A long lance was buried in the ground next to the chief. It was his weapon and a sign of his position in the tribe. They all waited patiently in silence. An infamous enemy was just about to ride right into their arms. Rusty didn't know it yet, but he was dropping a gift into Hachta's hands. He hoped his friend understood, but this man had to die.

The fire before the chief crackled and popped as cinders swirled skyward on thermal currents. Cotton-like clouds lazily crossed the sky as a light breeze whistled through the trees. A few vultures circled overhead, looking for scraps from the camp. The Indian dogs were already barking. They sensed the anticipation in the tribe, and they pulled at the ropes around their necks. Spears, bows, arrows, and tomahawks were seen in the warriors' hands. They knew exactly who they awaited and felt fortunate they had such an opportunity to seek revenge on such a demon of a man.

Hachta wondered what the Indian fighter was doing in the mountains and how he had found Rusty's compound. He knew how his friend was, and he fought hoof and tooth to keep the settlers off Crow land. The chief was very wise and understood the White men more than most Indians. As he spoke their language, it was harder for them to lie. When he occasionally encountered a White man he didn't know, he often acted like he couldn't understand, but he captured everything. He also understood the value of his friendship with Rusty Steel. They used him to barter and trade their furs, and he supplied them with axes, hatchets, knives, and metal pots hung over smoldering fires. Even their cooking utensils came from the grumpy old mountain man.

Hachta was quite aware of where all this was heading. He only hoped it happened after his lifetime. He only prayed for another decade of living like they had for thousands of years. He knew that in the future, none of them would live the same—if any were left alive. He was watching firsthand the demise of the bison. When they were gone, only Indian ghosts would roam the plains. Their ways would be no more. He would rather die than sit by and do nothing, accepting the inevitable.

He suddenly realized that maybe this was what the infamous major sought. Perhaps he was searching for his own demise. It must be hard to sleep knowing you've killed children with the excuse they would grow into enemies. The Army took their women and babies to the reservations, but most died on the trails.

No woman, child, or elder was visible in the camp. They had been ushered to the tents in the back near the narrow exit. When the famous Major Angry Eyes rode in, their husbands wanted them to be safe. He was famous for his trickery, so they had to be careful. Hachta's scouts hadn't seen any other soldiers in the mountains or even in the next valley below. It appeared, for some reason, he had come alone.

His new War Chief Niemba and the tribe's three medicine men sat beside Chief Hachta. Beside them were the tribe's elders. Behind them sat the warrior braves. It was an impressive sight. Over a hundred Indians covered in warpaint waiting to greet one of the most hated White men in the West. The chief thought the Indian gods must be looking down on them, chuckling at the folly that was about to unfold.

The Crow heard the crushing of icy snow as the mountain men climbed the trail. The softened sound of horses' hooves was unmistakable. They could smell fancy soap as soon as the wind shifted. It filled the air with the smell of White men. They knew the mountain men used lye soap, so it must be Angry Eyes.

Black and blond scalps hung from the chief's belt. He stood out from the rest due to his brace of flintlock pistols in his belt. A bow and a quiver of stone-head arrows were strapped across his back. He wore a loincloth above his knee-high moccasins. His face appeared to be chiseled in stone, and he was emotionless as he continued to stare, waiting for the folly from below to unfold. His hair was so black it almost had a blue tint and fell below his shoulders.

Red-winged blackbirds cawed. They were just about to fly south for the winter. They scratched at the light cover of snow, looking for worms and bugs. The Crow camp was so silent you could hear the horses pass gas; that, and the growing sound of those who approached. Horses occasionally whinnied and nickered as they climbed the last stretch to the stronghold. The sound of a mountain chickadee called out. Hachta tilted his head and returned the call.

Rusty Steel was the first man to lead his horse into the Crow Indian camp. He was on foot. It made them appear humbler in their approach. Hachta saw the surprise on his face when he saw all the warriors painted for war.

"Hold on just a minute now, there, Chief," Rusty said. "Whatcha gonna do? Kill us all? We just came for a friendly visit. I wanted to congratulate ya on becoming chief and all."

"You don't know who you have with you, Rusty Steel," Hachta said. "You have brought the devil to my home, to my people."

"You mean the major?" Rusty laughed. He wished it hadn't sounded so nervous. "Why, he's Will Forrester's uncle. Will's one of us, Hachta."

As Rusty continued to walk toward his friend, his confidence began to peel away like the skin of an onion. None of the braves looked at him. They all kept their piercing eyes on the major. He, in turn, scowled back at them. The major opened his mouth to say something, but Levi backhanded him, and he fell silent. Johnson towered over him and shook his fist in his face. Will's heart began to sink as he realized what they had done. He had a feeling his uncle had tricked them all. He was after the location of the Crow camp.

Steel looked around and said with furrowed brow, "You just give the word, and we'll be long gone like a turkey to the corn. It appears y'all be upset about somethin'."

By now, all nine men stood before the group of warriors and the chief, who was a force to be reckoned with. The chief stood, and they all stood with him. Rusty had fought the Blackfeet side by side with the chief, but now he felt things had changed. He shot a questioning glance at the major, who smiled in return. He looked like he was enjoying himself.

The Crow chief grumbled some words, and instantly, a dozen warriors fell on Angry Eyes. They were close enough that he couldn't grab his guns in time. He hadn't expected the whole camp to be waiting for his arrival.

They must fear me, Warren thought and smiled. They would fear him even more when he got away. Strangely enough, the man never considered that he might not be able to get out of the bind he was in now.

He immediately found himself bound hands and feet. Nobody was taking any chances with this soldier.

Hachta looked at Will and asked, "Rusty says this man is your family. He has the same blood as you?"

"Yes, sir, Chief Hachta," Will replied. "He's my uncle and came here to take me home."

"Do you know what the Plains Indians call your uncle?" Hachta asked, almost in a whisper.

"What do you mean, Chief?" Will asked, puzzled. "Do you know my uncle?"

"I don't know your uncle personally, but I know who this man is in front of us," Hachta said. "We call him Angry Eyes. He is the killer of children, women, and elders."

The major struggled against the rope and spat at the chief. His head was so red it looked like it would explode. "You might kill me, Chief, but I'll take you with me when you do," he snarled like a rabid dog.

"That's my uncle, Chief Hachta!" Will cried. "He didn't do anything to you. He's never been up hre in this part of the mountains that I know of. Isn't that right, Warren?"

"Will," Rusty growled. "Shut up, right now!" He turned to the chief and said, "I'm sorry about the youngin', Chief. He don't know the Indian ways when elders are talking. I'm teachin' 'em as fast as I can, so don't you worry. He won't be any bother."

"It's not the young Forrester I'm worried about—it's the major. You have very poor taste, my old friend. I am surprised you allowed this worm into your compound."

"Whatcha mean, worm?" Rusty asked, puzzled. "Do you know the major or somethin'? Do you know the chief, Warren? What in the heck is goin' on?"

"Don't believe anything they say!" the major barked. "They're no more than heathens."

"Excuse me, but I'm afraid I'm confused," Rusty said. "You're tryin' to tell me that the major is famous or somethin'?"

"The day you beat me will be the day the sun comes up backward!" the major roared.

"You're so noisy you sound like snowshoes with cowbells on 'em," Rusty spat. "The courtesy is limited to nitwits like you, Major, so keep your gob shut before I gag ya." He looked at the chief with questioning eyes.

"Major Warren Forrester is known to all the tribes on the plains," Hachta said. "We call him Angry Eyes because he looks so crazy when he's angry, and he's always angry. He kills young Indian boys, so they won't grow up to be enemies. If women and elders get in a crossfire, he kills them too. He has complete disregard for the Indian people. Not just Crow but Cheyenne, Sioux, Blackfeet, Ute, and even Comanche. There he didn't fare so well, did you, Major? This man is one of a half dozen of the biggest enemies to the Indian Nations. He is a butcher and tricked you into bringing him to the camp. He is wicked evil and wicked smart. I'm surprised he outsmarted you, Rusty Steel. You must be getting old."

"I ain't getting old, and he didn't outsmart me," Rusty retorted. "It was Levi who suggested he get to know some friendly Indians. He believed it would change his mind iffin he met y'all. Me, like him, didn't see any harm in trying to change a poor soul's mind."

"The only poor souls here are among you men," Hachta said, his mouth a gash. He pointed to the major's tied hands and feet in the dirt. "This is no man. He is a dog—no, he's worse than a dog. A dog is loyal."

TONKAWA

(Ten weeks earlier in Texas)

MAJOR WARREN FORRESTER LAUGHED WHEN HE HEARD what his stupid little nephew did. He was glad he had disgraced his father, and he had done it all on his own without the help of his wicked uncle. His brother had always thought himself better than Warren. He swore never to speak to him again when he was made general. He had been selected, and Warren had been passed over. He knew he was a better warrior than Will's father. But in the higher ranks of the military, it was more about politics than who you were and what you were capable of. The major was capable of following any and all orders no matter how vile they were.

He was just about to go out on another raid, but he intended to track down William as soon as they returned. He had heard about the Crow stronghold in the mountains for two years, so they showed no signs of moving on. It would be the perfect setting if he had a chance to kill the chief and maybe a medicine man or two. He wondered how many warriors could be in such a camp. How many Crow Indians could he kill with only fourteen men?

He had heard it was sizable, and till now, no one dared try to force them out. This was the opportunity Warren was waiting for. When they were done with the Tonkawa they had located there in Kansas, he would take his men and ride for the Rocky Mountains. It was late in the year, but his soldiers had endured all sorts of hardships, from desert storms to blizzards. He wouldn't let a little weather get in the way of locating the stronghold.

He rode, leading his fourteen men like he owned the land he traveled. With shoulders back and chin up, he glared at anybody they encountered unless they were Indians. Then they killed them as expeditiously as possible. The major often ordered his men to kill the defenseless with their bayonets or knives to save ammunition. He seemed to thrive on the Indians' suffering, and all in the name of the laws set out in Washington. Rather than ridicule, he got praise for what he did. He was one of the few famous Indian fighters on the plains. He never met a male Indian he didn't kill.

"Lieutenant!" the major shouted. "Get in here at once."

Lieutenant Beets raced into the officer quarters and stood to a rigid attention. He saluted the major with a jerk and stared straight ahead with his hat under his arm.

"Yes, sir, Major, sir," Beets replied.

The major had personally trained him, and he was ready at every beck and call. The lieutenant's mind was going about a million miles an hour, wondering if he had done something wrong.

"Let's move that patrol up to tomorrow," Major Forrester said. "There's word from our scouts that there's a Tonkawa camp nearby. The camp was so close I couldn't believe it. I have directions to the canyon, so we should be able to find it. They were hiding out in plain sight. I believe we can't let such an opportunity pass us by. We will assemble in the yard at oh-six-hundred. We should be able to find the canyon by the end of the day. We can study the situation at night and hit them first thing in the morning just like they do to us. At ease, Lieutenant."

The lieutenant breathed a sigh of relief. He never knew with the major if he was in trouble or not. He was known to fly off the handle and do some crazy things. But it was what it was. He was attached to him, and he dared not request a transfer. The major would take it personally and ruin him in the military. He was famous for doing such things to others too. He was a vengeful and deceitful man, and Beets didn't know anybody who liked him. That was a fact that didn't seem to bother Major Warren Forrester at all.

But the lieutenant also knew his brother was a powerful general back in Washington. Lieutenant Beets hoped somehow the major would put in a good word with the brass so he could rise in rank. He longed to be a captain, so he endured the verbal abuse and followed him into the most hellish journeys he never hoped to live again. Joe Beets kept telling himself he was only following orders, just like Major Forrester was following orders. That had been his crutch throughout his time participating in the Indian wars. He hoped to put it behind him soon and move on with his own frontier fort and command.

The following day, the fifteen men rode out at dawn. The leader gigged his big stallion, and they shot off for the Tonkawa camp that was supposed to be hidden in a canyon. There was only one way in and out, so it would be a turkey shoot if he could sneak up on them and watch them from above. As they rode, the major smiled when he thought about what would happen tomorrow morning if he was lucky. Lately, he had been lucky like that. Many opportunities to kill red men had appeared for him in the last weeks. The more he killed, the more reckless he became. His men noticed his change and wondered what would befall them all. Whatever the major did, they were the ones to feel the brunt of the violence.

That wasn't to say the major didn't fight his own battles. He was thrilled when he rode into combat against Indians. He carried four pistols in his belt, and long guns were sheathed one on either side of his saddle. He rode right into the middle of the mayhem with pistols blazing fire and smoke. This was when he felt most alive. It was the only time in his life he felt satisfied. He had been an unhappy child.

He blamed it on his brother. His parents claimed he was the most intelligent person in the family—living or dead. Warren never understood why they didn't see how bright he was. It was the same with his teachers. They, too, ignored his brilliant mind. He made sure his peers noticed him through his accomplishments.

Lieutenant Beets rode beside the major, and the other men rode in single file. They moved slower as they approached where his map said the camp would be. The major ordered his men to walk their horses while maintaining as low a profile as possible. The element of surprise was imperative.

The major raised his hand, and the patrol stopped. "It's right there," Major Forrester whispered. "See the two squaws walking toward the opening in the rocks? I doubt I'd have seen it if it weren't for the women. That's another brilliant stroke of luck, Beets. Before this is over, we'll be famous—that I can promise you."

"I sure do hope so, Major. Sometimes I feel like it's never gonna end." Beets didn't sound so sure of himself like his superior officer.

"End?" the major asked. He made a face like the word was distasteful. "There will always be a war to fight somewhere. What would we do without a war? I trust my country to keep me busy until my end. And even then, I want to go out in a blaze of glory with my boots on and my pistols spitting fire."

The major smiled as he imagined his glory-filled ending. The lieutenant frowned as he did the same.

"Send men out to check the layout of the Tonkawa camp," Major Forrester said. "I've got an idea that will make it easy, but I've got to know where their teepees are first. That, and make sure there's no way out. I'm going to take the rest of the patrol a mile back, so nobody runs into us. Once we know what we're looking at, I'll decide what we'll do."

They made a cold camp off the main trail and whispered when they spoke. The major's men were well-versed in killing Indians. They had been at it for some years with Forrester. Sure, some of them hadn't made it, but that was expected in the service. After a couple of hours, Beets returned.

He huddled with the major and said, "The teepees are all at the back. It makes them harder to see if someone wanders in. The entrance is only wide enough for a horse and rider, and there's no other way out."

"Fine," Forrester said as his eyes narrowed. "Get me a bow and arrow."

"A bow and arrow?" Beets asked. "Where am I supposed to find a bow and arrow?"

"Just find it, you fool," Forrester retorted. "Do your job, and don't ask so many stupid questions."

Yes, sir," Lieutenant Beets replied, then he turned and ran off.

They waited in the high buffalo grass for the lieutenant to return. The sun was already peeking over the horizon, making the sky blush like a rose. Cirrostratus streaked the sky, and there wasn't a breath of air.

Beets ran up out of breath. He tried to talk, but he gulped for air. Finally, he managed to give the major a bow with three arrows. Warren snatched them from his hands and didn't even ask him where he found them. The lieutenant's eyes shot daggers at his boss, but he never noticed. He had little concern about the personal opinions of his inferiors, so he paid little attention to how they viewed his orders, no matter how outlandish they were.

This order had Beets risking his life for the enjoyment of his superior officer. He'd snuck into the Tonkawa camp and stolen a small boy's bow and arrows that lay beside him as he slept. The lieutenant had never been so scared in his entire career, but he knew he had to comply with his orders. He didn't even want to imagine how it would be if he failed to do his job. He had heard old stories about the major shooting men for not fighting. Those tales stuck in his mind like glue. He never wanted to provoke such a thing from the major.

"Get me a lantern and some bandages," Forrester ordered. He watched as Beets caught his breath and said impatiently, "Are you still here?" Warren's eyes shot daggers at his first officer.

Before the sun was clear of the horizon, the arrows were ready. The major leaped astride his horse and raced for the canyon. Beets followed, struggling to keep up. The men looked at each other, confused. Then they all took off after the boss, although he rode off without giving them orders. Nobody said a word, but they knew they had to follow the major. No matter what his orders were.

In no time, he and Beets were scaling the side of the mountain to where they could see the camp below them. The first breakfast fires were lit, and smoke squirreled toward the sky. The camp seemed sleepy, and the Indians were lazy to get moving after a sound night's sleep. Teepees dotted the back of the small canyon. Some thirty or forty people moved lazily around the Indian camp. A corral of Indian ponies held two dozen skinny horses.

It was obvious these Tonkawa Indians were as poor as church mice. One Indian led a horse from the corral and took it to the other side of the camp. There it was killed, butchered and split up between the warriors' families. They were so poor they were eating their horses. The major sneered at the penniless Indians with distain. He knew he was doing his country a great service, ridding them of the savages as effectively as he possibly could. He considered them to be below White men and even below horses and mules. Major Forrester thought of them as no more than beasts of the wilderness.

Beets sniffed the air and smelled the kerosene-soaked bandages. They were wrapped around the arrows' shafts just below the arrowhead.

"Light them up, mister." The major smiled, and his eyes twinkled with wickedness. He pulled back the bowstring and sent the arrows sailing into the sky. The moon cast a gray tint on everything as stars twinkled in the heavens.

Three flaming arrows flew in arcs across the canyon, landing in the heavy brush at the camp's entrance. It was the end of summer, and everything was dry and brittle. As soon as the burning arrows hit the bushes and small trees, they burst into flames like a bomb. Black smoke billowed as flames leaped into the sky and women and children screamed. It spread quickly as it raced for the other end of the camp. The Indians were cowering in the corner as the smoke got thicker.

Down in the canyon, there wasn't the slightest breeze. The major and lieutenant both felt the heat as it rose from the burning inferno below them. The smoke stung their eyes and made them water. Still, the major watched motionlessly as the humans in the camp below them burned alive.

Lieutenant Beets gasped in shock. Children ran all around the Tonkawa stronghold trying to escape the unescapable flames. Mothers screamed as they dragged their children and tried to claw their way up the canyon wall. None of them had thought to keep the area free of debris in case there was a fire. They thought it would give them more cover, hoping not to be discovered. Major Forrester's plan had worked perfectly. Every man, woman, and child were killed to the very last one.

The soldiers hadn't even aimed their weapons at the enemy. The major had single-handedly murdered the entire tribe down to the last baby. He felt he had just made a significant accomplishment. There weren't very many Tonkawa left. He may have just eliminated his first tribe. The act made him feel good inside, and it wasn't because he was complying with his orders. This he did all on his own and he would claim all the recognition.

Major Forrester led his men cautiously into the camp the following day. The ground was too hot to ride in right after the fire. Now, they were there to inspect the damage they had wreaked on the small Tonkawa village. The burned and charred corpses lay scattered across the camp. Not a teepee was left standing. Many mothers had died with their children in their arms. Their faces were frozen into masks of pain and fear. Those were the ones that weren't burned to a crisp. Others seemed to not have a scratch. Those were the ones at the back who had succumbed to the thick smoke. Many lay in each other's arms, and warriors lay with bows and arrows in their hands, but they didn't even have a chance to save themselves or defend their families.

"Make sure you get an accurate account of the numbers dead, Lieutenant," the major said as he inspected each corpse. He had a crazy smile frozen on his face. "Just count the heads. There's no need to distinguish sexes and sizes. As you take the numbers, make sure you have a couple of the men take their ears to take back to the fort. We usually take scalps, but today they're too burned up. The ears should snap right off. That will be positive confirmation of our kills. I don't want to be cheated out of a single body. Do you understand, Beets?"

The lieutenant gulped down his disgust and said, "Yes, sir, Major, sir."

The lieutenant's mind was going a hundred miles per hour as he tried to deal with the slaughter he had just witnessed. It had all happened so fast that it wasn't until the blazing inferno was upon the Indians that he realized what the major had planned. By then, it was too late to try to reason. Then again, he didn't see the point. There was no arguing with a madman. It was obvious to Lieutenant Beets. He only hoped their men didn't notice. It was bad enough for one of their officers to be mad. He just hoped he could hold on to his own sanity.

"Did you see that, Lieutenant?" Major Warren Forrester asked, obviously happy. "We cleaned out the whole camp and didn't fire a single bullet. That's a first even for me. Go back and get our men so they can see this. It was genius, if I have to say so myself."

He smiled so wide it looked like his face would break. He didn't notice the panic and terror on his lieutenant's face. He never cared what his subordinates thought or felt. He assumed they thought he was brilliant, just like he believed. Had he turned around and seen the fourteen men's faces, he would have been shocked. Now, they too knew he was mad, and there wasn't a thing they could do about. If they deserted Major Forrester, they knew they would get a bullet for their efforts. Nobody ran off on their boss. Not alive anyway.

One man silently cried openly at the murder of small children and even babies. Blood pooled beneath bodies, and others were burned to a crisp. The ones that died from smoke inhalation were the strangest. They seemed to be in various stages of waking up and preparing breakfast. Fires still smoked around the camp as dozens of streams of smoke rose into the air after everything was burned. All that was left was scorched earth. The major seemed to be enjoying himself so much that he never shot a curious look over his shoulder. He stared ahead with a look of glee on his face. Beets wondered if he wasn't completely insane, or was he a psychopathic murderer? Not even a crazy person would be capable of what he had just done. It was an abomination.

After the massacre at the Tonkawa stronghold, the major rode back to the fort with his fourteen men. He was proud of the fact he didn't have a single casualty. Dozens of ears hung from the neck of one of the pack mules as they dried. Blow flies hovered over the bloody flesh and cartilage. As the cavalry patrol pressed forward, horses' hooves hammered the earth as dirt corkscrewed into the air behind them. A cloud of dust followed everywhere they went. The major wasn't worried about being seen by the enemy.

He happily invited any challenge from any and all to try to defeat him and his men in battle. At this point, he was so successful in eliminating the red race that he felt empowered and even entitled. He knew what he was accomplishing would be praised back in Washington and even back at his fort. He was a hero to those who heard the stories secondhand. Those that were there were too shy and nervous to even talk about it.

When they rode into the fort, they got the news. The Texas Rangers were trailing a war party from West Texas numbering as many as a hundred Comanche warriors as they raced east toward the cities of Central Texas. The minute the major got the message, he had his men change for fresh horses, and they rode out two hours later. As they pressed their animals southward, Major Forrester kept his eyes straight ahead, ignoring his worn-out troops' discomfort. For him, there was no distance too far to ride if it meant more success in the Indian wars.

As they rode south for the Red River, the Texas Rangers along with the Texan militia were dogging the Comanche led by Buffalo Hump, the most feared Comanche of them all. He was a warrior leader and not even a chief, but more Indians followed him on his raid for revenge than any other Indian during the war with the original inhabitants of the country.

The major felt lucky with the defeat of the Tonkawa. Maybe he could add a Comanche war party to that. He intended to become the terror of the Western Plains. Every Indian alive would fear his name. He had heard the Indians had even given him a name, and he loved it. The more fame he acquired, the more juice he would have back East. Hopefully, more than even his general brother.

They rode long hard days, pressing the horses as much as they could as they raced south to assist the Rangers and militia. The men were used to their major pushing them beyond most men's limits, but then again, they were still alive. They gave the credit for that to their crazy superior officer, Major Warren Forrester.

THE CHASE

When the major finally caught up with the Texan militia, they joined their ranks, later hooking up with the Texas Rangers that had been dogging the hostiles' trail. The major took the size of the war party in stride because he was riding with a group of hardened Indian fighters, and they had superior weapons. By now, the Comanche war party led by Buffalo Hump was more than five hundred warriors strong and growing as they roared across the plains.

Part of the war party broke off and headed for Victoria. Now, even the major was shocked at the sheer size of the band of warriors from several tribes. They raced across the center of Texas, killing every White man, woman, and child in their path. Nobody tried to stop them because it was an impossible task. The handful of Rangers, militia and Army soldiers was terribly outnumbered by the massive Comanche war party. They killed and burned their way across the state, headed for the big prize.

Major Forrester was all for following them into the

town to kill them all. The Texas Ranger Captain was in charge, and he ordered them to stand their ground and wait. Three hundred more Comanche were waiting not too far away. They now found themselves sandwiched in the middle, so they hunkered down and waited. When they heard the town citizens returning rifle and pistol fire, the Indians gathered what they had stolen, loaded it onto mules, and emptied the town corrals and stables. Finally, they roared out of the town the same way they came in.

The Texas Ranger ordered his men to hold fire. The Indians were retreating, so he didn't see the need to risk the lives of his men until he had a better picture of the entirety of the war party. Now, they were more than six hundred strong. By the time they hit Linnville, there were a thousand painted warriors and Indian ponies. They attacked the city with such ferocity that the Ranger Captain again told them to show restraint. He didn't want him and his men to be wiped out. Captain Burns knew they didn't have a chance against a force so large and obviously well organized.

Weeks before the raid, the Texas Rangers had thirty-three Comanche captives and bartered with the Indians to trade several chiefs and their families for captive White women and children. This was the first of the peace negotiations with the hostile tribe. When the Comanche had arrived with only one White girl, sixteen-year-old Matilda Lockhart, they were infuriated. They expected an equal number. In a rage, some Texas Rangers murdered the Indian captives with their wives and families—even the elder chiefs were shot down where they stood.

It was a slaughter brought on by a lack of understanding. Matilda was the only White captive they could find. For some reason, the Texas Rangers thought they held as many captive whites as they did Indians. When they brought a single White girl to complete the exchange, the Texans' anger soured, and accusations were exchanged. Then one of the Texas Rangers shot one of the captive Indians, and they all pulled their guns and wasted everybody. A cacophony of bullets riddled the bodies of the prisoners.

When Buffalo Hump heard of the slaughter, which came during what were supposed to be peace talks, he rode to all the nearby tribes. He united past enemies to fight against their new common enemy, the White men. Every Indian in Texas and some outside the state had heard of the betrayal. Still, no White man was charged. The captives didn't even have weapons when they were brutally shot and murdered. Nobody even made an excuse. It was just another slaughter, like many past and more to come.

Of course, they didn't know it, but they were witnessing "The Great Comanche Raid"—the most significant attack on White settlers and citizens in Indian history. Some said it was because the Indians lusted for White men's possessions. But those who were there knew it was about revenge. The raid was for killing their chiefs for no apparent reason other than rage. There would have been nothing less to cause the tribes to unite as one and attempt to force the White men from Texas. They swept across the land like a hurricane, erasing homes, farms, and ranches on their way westward.

Finally, Texas Ranger Burns yelled, "Let's go get 'em, boys!" The Rangers and militia raced forward.

The fourteen soldiers looked at their officer for orders. Warren stared at the Rangers angrily as they gained distance. The head Ranger hadn't even discussed the decision with the major. He would show them what he was made of if it was the last thing he ever did.

"Charge!" Warren shouted as he gigged his stallion's bloody flanks with pointed spurs, and they shot off like a bullet.

The Texas Rangers had cleverly waited until the Comanche tried to turn around and run for home with all they had stolen. But they found the mules they used to carry the silver and valuables made them vulnerable to the sporadic but accurate gunfire to their rear. The mules and a few thousand head of horses were slowing them down. As they raced westward, the Rangers, militia, and Army patrol ran behind them, nipping at their heels.

The horses' lungs sounded like steam engines as they were pressed to their limits. The major's stallion rode out in front of the pack, racing for the rear of the retreating Comanche. His men came, urging their horses to run faster behind their boss. The Texas Rangers kept back but within rifle range and picked the Comanche off one at a time. In minutes, thirty warriors or horses hit the dirt. The White men chasing them were deadly shots, both with their rifles and with their pistols.

Finally, it looked like the Comanche had given up. Two thousand horses and mules were let loose to wander across the trail. It looked like they broke away from the herd or were abandoned. But the major saw their victory wasn't guaranteed yet. The warriors continued to flee for Central Texas and their hidden stronghold. He still had time to kill again as many as they had already killed. Later, they would return to take their scalps and trophies. The major prided himself in providing proof of his work, and he loved the acknowledgment.

The militia found the bullion stolen from both Victoria and Lynnville. They and the Texas Rangers immediately split the silver up, but Major Forrester had already ridden off, hot on the trail of the Comanche. If he could kill Buffalo Hump, he would reach the fame he sought. Then, his peers would have to take notice. He felt he was the best commander and bravest officer in the Indian wars. He wasn't interested in money. His family had plenty. He was interested in power and recognition of a career that, till now, seemed to have gone unnoticed and stalled.

Once the Rangers and militia had split up their plunder, they turned around and headed back home one and all. Now, with the Comanche on the run and having captured the silver, they figured their job was finished.

As his soldiers raced forward, Major Forrester drew his saber, raised it in the air, and screamed, "Charge!" They ran through a thin line of Comanche into Buffalo Hump's trap. Hundreds of arrows flew through the air. They hovered over them like a storm cloud before raining down on the soldiers. Ten men were killed in the first barrage. Forrester raged against the Comanche, riding into the middle of a group of warriors and slashing at them with his sword.

He looked so wild and crazy it gave the Indians pause, and they didn't kill him even though they had plenty of chances. It was bad medicine to kill the

insane. They could all see it in the officer's eyes. Even
his few remaining men saw it. It was Angry Eyes, and he
had gone off the rails. Blood spatter covered his face and
body as he hacked with his sword at anything within
reach. Even his men steered clear of the madman killing
machine.

Suddenly, Warren found himself wheeling his horse
in circles, looking for the enemy, but they were all gone.
He turned to his men to order another charge, but all
but four were dead, and three were wounded. Only
Lieutenant Beets remained unscathed. He looked like
one of the dead. He was pale, as the blood had drained
from his face. He looked at his commanding officer with
the strangest expression and with hollow, empty eyes.
He mouthed something to his boss, but no words came.
They locked eyes for an instant, and what Beets saw
terrified him. He felt a cold chill shatter his soul.

Right then and there, Lieutenant Beets decided he
was done. He tipped his hat to his men and turned and
walked away. He had finally decided to quit the major.
His boss saw he was walking away, and it put him in a
rage.

"If you take another step, I'll shoot you myself, Lieutenant Beets!" Forrester shouted.

The major's face was red from blood and anger and
a blue vein pulsated on his forehead. That was the last
thing Beets saw before he walked a hundred yards away,
pulled his pistol, cocked the hammer, and blew his
brains out. His body fell to the ground, and he died
instantly. His nightmares and sins died with him.

Of course, the soldiers left were shocked to their
very core. They struggled to cope with what had
happened in the last few days. They had gone from

some kind of evil glory and victory at the Tonkawa hideout to the sound of whooping Comanche as they raced across Texas on their path of revenge.

The Army survivors followed their major as they returned to the nearest frontier fort. The men rode on wounded horses and limped their way back home. Strangely, the man who took the most risks didn't have a scratch on him, and he felt victorious even in the light of the loss of his patrol. Not a single man came out without a cut or bruise except the major. Still, the Comanche heathen failed to kill him. At this point, he almost felt immortal—even invincible.

When they returned to the frontier fort, the major sent his men to the doctor and headed for his quarters. There, he found a letter. He scowled when he read who it was from. It said General Daniel Forrester in gold letters—his fancy-pants brother. They hadn't spoken for years. He wondered what he might want after all this time. They had sworn to never speak to each other again as long as they lived.

The major's first impulse was to wad it up and throw it in the trash. He went to his desk and rifled the rest of his mail. Then, he paused as he pondered the letter from his brother, the big-shot general. Maybe there was news of something vital, although he couldn't think of what that might be. He stood, walked over to the garbage can, and pulled the envelope out. He sat again and used his hands to flatten the wrinkled letter, then opened it with a thin letter knife. It was short but to the point. The contents made the major laugh.

The gears in his brain began to churn, and a plan began to form. He knew there had to be several ways he could use this information against his brother. He couldn't believe he had written him asking for help. Who did he think he was? First, he should have apologized. The major couldn't give a rat's tail about his brother. He hated him with a passion. As for little William, he could hardly remember the brat. He hated children and avoided them whenever possible.

Just the same, the major saw the information as important. He might be able to get even with his brother and at the same time get the recognition he desired. He didn't want a higher rank now that he found how much he liked battle and combat, but still, if his name and picture were on the front page of every newspaper in the nation, they would have to admit they were wrong for not giving him more important details.

With the lack of clear orders, Forrester took it upon himself to take the fight to the Indians rather than have him and his men sit on their laurels and wait to be attacked. Now, he began to make up his own plans that fit his agenda. He planned to put himself in a position that would shame his brother. Maybe if he was lucky, he would be able have him busted back to a colonel. He snickered to himself and continued to scheme.

UNCLE WARREN

UNITED STATES CAVALRY MAJOR WARREN FORRESTER rode out of the fort on his own. He had lost eleven men and had three more wounded. One probably wouldn't make it, so the major had to wait on a new detail to be attached to his command. Replacements were always a problem, and he felt he didn't have the time to waste, nor could he let this opportunity pass him by. If he did, he would get no revenge against his brother.

When his replacements were assigned, he would continue his battle against the local Indians. But first, he had some serious business to do. He had a long ride ahead of him. It was said that the deserter, Captain William Forrester, was hiding in the mountains near a large Crow camp. He thought he could combine some enjoyment with work and kill two frogs with one stone.

If he could locate the camp and get away to come back with his army, he could wipe out a major stronghold. Then he would be in the newspapers like he hoped. He would have done something nobody else could do, especially not his cowardly sibling. He hated him even more than he hated the red skins.

He headed for Colorado and the foothills of the Rocky Mountains. His skills were not those of a mountain man, but he believed he knew enough to survive. He had outlived many he knew, sleeping rough every night and fighting most days. He wondered if he could single-handedly kill the chief and a few medicine men. Maybe he could take a bit of the fight out of them before returning with a hundred men armed to the teeth with pistols, rifles, and small cannon. He could pack them on mules and assemble them at the Crow camp and blow the Indians to smithereens.

As he rode into the mountains, the first snow fell around him. He pulled his bearskin coat up around his ears and his hat down over his eyes and rode on. He was a soldier and was used to riding for long distances with little rest. Their job was to chase down wild Indians to kill or send to the reservation. That night, he pulled his bedroll over his head and comfortably slept on. He no longer feared any Indians, so he built a fire to keep him warm. He believed that even if they captured him, he could get away.

His mind was like a steel trap and sharp as a razor. All he had to do was use his nephew to find out where the large Crow camp was. Then, with his brilliant intellect, he would decide the fastest way to eliminate the enemy. He wondered what a Crow Indian looked like. Then again, it didn't matter to him. If they were red, he considered them dead in his sick mind.

He thought back on the times he'd visited his brother. There hadn't been over a dozen in the last twenty years. He hadn't even remembered the runt until he read what he did in the newspapers. Then, his memory was jolted, and he could vaguely remember going to visit, and his brother's son wore a military school uniform. The face of the young man was vague, but the stab at his ego he remembered was as clear as a ship's bell at night—Will had gotten into West Point and Warren didn't. Even with his father's connections, Warren's grades weren't good enough to get in West Point. That was another beef he had with his snob of a brother, the general.

The next morning, he followed the trail marked with an X on the crude map his brother had acquired and forwarded to him. It was all hearsay, so he wasn't even sure if he would be there, but he didn't have enough men to stage a patrol, so if he had to wait anyway, he might as well wait while having a little fun.

Although the trail was covered in an inch of snow with small drifts of a foot, he could tell the path he followed was well-traveled. The farther he rode, the more confident he became that he was on the right road to some small compound of three houses deep in the Rocky Mountains. He wondered how his nephew ran off the rails—especially a man who was said to have a significant future ahead of him. His grades at school were said to be straight A's, and he'd requested a post on the frontier forts and the Indian wars.

He remembered his blond hair and bright blue eyes as it all came back to him. He was even a handsome young fellow, much like Warren was before he became scarred up and when his eyes weren't scary. He rubbed his hand across a six-day stubble of beard and wondered how he looked. Then again, he doubted there were many beauty contests in the mountains.

He pulled his horse and mule to a stop at a stream and dismounted. His animals refreshed themselves while Warren scrubbed his face with soap he brought from camp. He was shocked when he looked at his reflection in the cold water. He had changed so much these last months that he looked like another person. He debated on whether he should shave or not. Then again, he wasn't riding into a fort or a military compound. Maybe his rugged look would fit in more with the strange people who chose to live in the wilderness much like the very Indians he was fighting to eliminate.

He wondered if his nephew would remember his face, and he wondered if he would remember his. If he lived in the mountains, he must be living like Indians. How did a Forrester with such a lineage of military men make such a drastic change for the worst? A West Point man, no less. If Warren had been sent to West Point rather than his nephew, he would have graduated at the head of his class, and it wouldn't be learning how to make maps—it would be military strategy.

Small fish swam lazily around the bottom as he looked in the water. He wondered where they went when everything froze. He made camp by the stream that night. The tinkle of water was soothing, allowing him a nightmare-free evening. He slept close to the fire as the cinders glowed orange on his face. Asleep, he looked like any other soldier—maybe a decent human being. But as soon as he awoke, he would put the monster's face back on again and continue his journey through life, wreaking the wrath on every enemy he encountered.

The following day, he stoked the fire to heat his

hands enough to make breakfast. It was still snowing lightly, making everything clean and white. Despite the breathtaking beauty, the major noticed nothing. He only enjoyed his job and ignored the rest of the world as it passed him by. He mechanically prepared the same meal he had twice a day—pork and beans. For lunch, he kept riding and chewed on hard tack.

He filled his stomach with the usual and a small kettle of thick black coffee. He wondered if today would be the day he found William. He was looking forward to the look of shame that he knew would be on his face when his family caught him out by surprise. He chuckled to himself at the thought. He even smiled, but what reached his eyes was something cruel and devious. If you ignored the smile you could see how evil the major had become.

He unhobbled his horse, saddled it up, and grabbed the lead to the mule. They continued to ride into the mountains, higher all the time. As they climbed, the temperatures dropped, but the bearskin kept him warm. Another day without seeing another living thing and another warm and quiet night. On the last night, he wondered if he was on a wild goose chase. Maybe his brother was playing a trick on him, and he had fallen for it, hook, line, and sinker. He wondered how many days he should continue to travel. He knew bad weather was on its way, but he had slept rough in every kind of weather, including hail and rain. A little Rocky Mountain weather wasn't about to scare him off.

The next day, he rode through what he took for a cemetery of some sort. Indian bodies lay on six-foot platforms in the blazing sun. When he arrived, a few vultures and a dozen crows took flight. It smelled like blood. Or rain, or stagnant water—something almost swampy.

Finally, in the distance, he saw three lines of smoke squirrel into the sky. That matched the claim of three cabins. He knew not to expect much from a bunch of hermits that lived isolated in the mountains. Who knows what kind of people William got mixed up with? He wondered how his nephew had gotten this far off the path he and his father had chosen for him as an infant. From the day William was born, his brother planned for his military career, and of course, Warren felt the same back then. Now, he didn't really know how he felt, or maybe it was that he just didn't care anymore. He felt like he was on the road to destruction. But the destruction of whom? Him or the heathens?

He knew he didn't care what William had done or planned to do. Although he would like to see him shamed in front of his brother, the general. He imagined bringing him back—a White man turned Injun. His brother would have a heart attack just at the sight of him. Maybe it would be worth taking him back too. Maybe it would all work out in his favor. He imagined in his sick mind the shock on his brother's face when he saw what his son had become.

Maybe he had gone too far and wouldn't want to leave the Indian way of life. He had heard of it happening. But mostly with women who were captured and later didn't want to leave their husbands and children when they were rescued from the life they had eventually adopted.

Things always went Warren's way, so he wasn't worried. He had gotten himself into all kinds of jams during the years fighting the Indians, and he had worked his way out of every one. Some said he had the luck of the devil, and others said he had made a pact. Of course, he lost men—scores of them—more men than all the other patrols combined, but he also hit more objectives and successfully completed more difficult orders than any other officer. Of that he was proud. For some reason, the number of men lost mattered little to the power-hungry killer.

When the military had a dirty job or something too dangerous, they always sent Warren. The commanding officers knew whatever they asked him to do, he would get it done one way or the other. His methods were brutal, but there were such men in every war.

He had the Indians on the run in Texas, so he believed he could do the same thing in the mountains. He knew for a fact the Crow Indians weren't as fierce as the Comanche. Anybody that had fought them could confirm that. Their war cries brought goosebumps on Warren's arms whenever he heard them. But the fear was part of the pleasure too. There was nothing like the feeling of winning a battle and finding you had survived unscathed. That moment when your body was so pumped up on adrenaline you felt you would explode. That, too, was part of the addiction.

The iron shoes on the stallion slipped on the icy trail while the mule never missed a step. Still, Warren knew he had to ride into the camp on his horse like he always did—just like he owned the place. He stopped and listened carefully. He could smell burning wood, but all he heard was the breeze whistling through the pine needles on the trees. Despite sighting the smoke, he wondered because it was so deep in the forest that he couldn't see anything living there but grizzly bears.

He touched his horse's flanks. It, too, bore battle scars like its master. It was a similar animal to its master. It, too, only had one speed: full speed. It also attacked like it had blinders on and drove deep into enemy lines. He even believed his horse felt the adrenaline rush just like him when they clashed with the warriors. Warren's heart hammered in his chest as he thought of past battles. He believed this journey would take him to that violent place where he had lived many days.

His horse struggled the last bit of the climb, where the path narrowed even more. Then he found himself in a clearing with a wooden zig-zag fence around it. Seven horses raced around the stables, but there were eight mules. He wondered if there was a hidden eighth horse. He was razor-sharp and didn't miss anything. He saw the ruffians sitting at a table on one of the cabin's porches.

The major rode right up to the house uninvited. He knew this would put them on the defensive. He wanted to make it clear who was boss here. His horse pranced as the officer looked down his nose at the six men on the porch. He saw several revolvers on the tables and rifles leaning against the building. If he wasn't mistaken, they knew he was coming even though he hadn't seen any Indians or White spies.

He wondered if they might know more about the wilderness than he did. He stared down at the men and then spat a half yard of tobacco juice to the side. Suddenly, dark, hollow pistol barrels pointed his way as hammers clicked loud in the silence. He blinked, smiled, and ignored the men as he threw his leg over his horn and slid off his horse. His boots crushed ice when they landed in the snow.

CHIEFS & WARRIORS

THE MOUNTAIN MEN STOOD TO ONE SIDE AND THE CROW warriors to the other. Smoke squirreled skyward from a dozen fires across the Indian camp. Major Warren Forrester sat in the middle. He watched the Indians carefully, probably looking for a chance to escape. He was still confident that he would prevail despite being tied hands and feet. He still didn't see that he had been defeated without a shot fired—just like back at the Tonkawa camp.

But Levi didn't believe it was a possibility. Even if he did get away, they could easily find him. They had known well ahead of his arrival that he was coming. Hachta's people probably knew it when he walked into the forest and began climbing the mountains. There were no secrets kept from the Indians that populated the Rocky Mountains.

"What's gonna happen now, Rusty?" Will whispered.

"I have no idea," Steel replied. "I figure iffin we're lucky, we'll leave with our scalps. That uncle of yours has turned out to be an evil man. It's odd how that happens. You came out as right as rain, and your father's brother is as wicked a man as ever walked the plains, according to what Hachta told me about him. I'm afraid I can't save 'im, Will. Don't take it too hard. He was planning to do you in and all. What do you think would have been waiting for you back East were you to return with your uncle?

"I'd say he has a mean streak in him ten miles long," Rusty continued. "With him being so infamous with the Indians, he's not long for this world. I wonder what made him think he could just waltz into a Crow stronghold with his reputation and survive? It was like he was teasing luck, or his destiny, or somethin'. Or maybe he's looking for the brave man's way out. If he killed himself, he'd just be another coward. But if he dies at the hands of his enemies, he will have died a hero in his eyes." Rusty doubted many more people saw him as a hero, though.

"So, what happens now, Chief Hachta?" Rusty asked as he turned toward the warriors. Hostile eyes shot daggers at all the White men. Rusty wasn't feeling so sure of himself just then.

He wanted to get things moving one way or another. Now, all he wanted was for the eight mountain men to be allowed to return to their cabin in the forest. What happened to the major was something they couldn't stop without risking their lives and surely being thrown off the mountain. They couldn't stand up to so many warriors. Would they be inclined to let them go, knowing they had brought Major Warren Forrester to their camp? Rusty wondered what he had been thinking. He was no more than a psychopath who enjoyed killing. As an Army major, he could do so legally. He had a license to kill and didn't use it sparingly.

Hachta had been staring mesmerized at the Army major that so much Indian gossip was about. He was considered the evilest White man in the Army. They had already heard about the massacre in the Tonkawa camp. They were the Crow's enemies and always had been, but that didn't mean they condoned what the major did. He burned them like cowards rather than fighting them like the noblemen the warriors were. He even killed the babies. Then, it was said, he rode down to inspect his handiwork. He was proud of his actions as he committed genocide on the Native American Indians.

The chief turned his head toward his old friend and gave him a small smile, but it didn't reach his eyes. His blood brother had unwittingly brought a vile enemy right into their camp. The chief didn't know whether to reward them for bringing him to them or to throw them off the mountain for doing something so foolish. Either way, the major wouldn't leave there alive. His ashes would swirl skyward after the Crow Indians slowly turned him back to dust.

"You let me loose for five minutes, and I'll cut all your throats," the major hissed like a snake. He struggled fruitlessly with his bindings. He seemed to be convinced he somehow had the upper hand. What could a man like that do in the position he was in? Rusty had a sneaking suspicion that the major had never been on the wrong side of a whip. He had never been admonished for his butchery. He was rewarded instead, even when he brought in the scalps of his enemies to prove the numbers he claimed to have killed. He relished in the fact he always brought proof.

"You're the only man I've ever met that can put both of your feet in your mouth at the same time," Rusty spat at the major. "Don't you think you're in enough trouble already?"

"You don't believe these heathens can kill me, do you?" the major growled.

"Ya can pert near count on it, Major," Rusty replied. "And I wouldn't help you if you were in church prayin'."

"What do you want me to do?" Warren asked. His face was distorted by his hatred. "Say I'm sorry for killing Indians?"

"That sounded about as sincere as a five-dollar funeral, mister," Angus said.

Without a word, the chief cut the bindings that held the major's feet. Now he could stand. Without the slightest warning, Levi hit the major with a haymaker. He didn't knock him down, but he made his knees wobble. He rubbed his jaw and spat a glob of blood. He smiled with a mouthful of red teeth. He fished around in his mouth with his tongue and spat out a molar.

"You better have the law on your side," the major said to Levi. "Hitting a military officer is a court-martial offense. Come on then, try again. As big as you are, and you didn't even knock me down."

"Even if I don't have the law on my side, I'm big enough to get away with it," Levi said. "You tried to use my friend to get at the Crow camp, and you'd probably take your own blood back to prison just because you could."

"Hur, hur, hur." Warren chuckled. "Cut my hands,

and I'll tear you to pieces, big boy. I cut men down like you like I chop down trees. The same goes for you, Chief Hachta. Yeah, I know who you are. Why do you think I used my worthless nephew to find your camp? All eight of them men are fools and cowards."

"Luck is with you today, Rusty Steel," Hachta said. "I am going to allow you to go back to your cabins. I know you didn't do this to bring my people harm. But you did it just the same. You wouldn't be walking away from our camp if we weren't blood brothers. Consider yourselves lucky."

"What ya gonna do with this scoundrel?" Rusty asked. He looked at Will, but his eyes were full of hate. His uncle had shown his true colors, and his nephew felt no remorse.

"You better worry about yourself and yours," Chief Hachta said. "Like I said, you are free to leave. I would hurry if I were you. Some of my warriors aren't going to like what I'm doing. Now go, all of you. I don't want to see you again this winter. Go back to your cabins, trap for beaver, and forget about this fool. He's already dead —he just doesn't know it yet."

By the time they returned to the compound, a full moon had broken out over the horizon, casting an eerie gray tint over the country. Back at the Crow camp, the major's eyes were wild and angry. His face was iridescent in the moonglow. He was tied to stakes on the ground face up. When he saw the moon, he howled like a wolf, snapping his teeth, and spat and growled at anyone who got close. Major Forrester was entirely out of his mind. Still, he struggled at his bindings. Hachta walked over to the spread-eagle body. He pulled back his bow line and sent an arrow through the major's hand deep into the dirt. He did the same with his other hand and then his feet. Blood pooled in the major's palms.

THE JOURNEY

LEVI JOHNSON MOUNTAIN MAN
SCOUT 8

It seems to be a law of nature, inflexible and inexorable, that those who will not risk cannot win.

John Paul Jones

TRAPPER WARS

LEVI BEAVER JOHNSON AND EX-CAPTAIN WILLIAM Forrester carefully waded waist-deep into the freezing stream with their rifles in their white-knuckled fists. They each had their brace of pistols over their shoulders to keep the powder dry. Every few minutes, they stopped and listened while taking a deep breath.

They sought out scents, sounds, or motions that could indicate danger. Their hearts hammered between their ears as they crept toward the thieves. They knew they were outnumbered, so the element of surprise was essential. Levi counted five pairs of White men's boots.

These men were no challenge for Levi to follow, especially in the winter with the first solid snowfall. When he was a boy, it was said he could track a snake across a river. He had tracked and hunted all his life back in Southeastern Indiana in the forest where his family still lived. Back home, they had even given him the nickname of Trapper Boy and later Beaver for his skills. Johnson was also the best shot in the Rockies. It was doubted Rusty Steel could beat him anymore. He had a better gun than when he'd arrived and entered his first competition, and with it, he'd become an even better shot.

They'd begun tracking the thieves as soon as they found their pelts stolen. They could hardly believe more White men were spending the winter in the freezing temperatures of the Rockies. Men willing to risk their lives to acquire the valued cold-water pelts they paid so much for back in New York and Boston. The one thing he was sure of was that the tracks they saw weren't Indians. They wore White men's heavy boots.

When they got close enough to hear them talk, they waded along the water's edge as they moved close to the shore. The clicks of hammers—they carefully moved forward with their guns ready. Then the bushes rustled, and Levi put his arm out to stop Will from moving forward. He nodded to the rustling trees. They pressed themselves into the snowdrifts at the stream's bank.

As more men moved toward the poachers, branches moved, and small globs of snow fell to the ground. They couldn't see them, but they could follow their path by the movement of the snow-covered vegetation. They heard their footsteps in the frosted snow as they came closer.

Still, the White men spoke as a trail of smoke rose from their fire. They weren't even trying to hide like they should be, especially after poaching the beaver furs from somebody's traps. In the wilderness, it was a killing offense. The only law in the Rocky Mountains was what they made themselves. It was the law of respect for other men with similar lives. There was little tolerance for thieves—predominantly White men who took what wasn't theirs.

When the first Blackfoot warrior showed up, both men were shocked. On this journey, they had yet to have much contact with the Indians from the Rocky Mountains, and during the last months, they hadn't encountered any Indians, especially ones painted like these.

Will cupped his hand and whispered into Levi's ear. "What do you think?"

"I reckon we're between a roaring river and a cliff, pard," Levi whispered. "We've got Blackfeet warriors on the other side of the stream and our five poachers on this side. The problem is we're in the middle, and if we move now, the Indians will see us for sure. I doubt the White men know any of us are even here. They must be as dumb as mud."

"We're all in for a surprise any moment now," Will said in a barely audible voice.

More than speaking, they were reading each other's lips. Their eyes locked, full of questions and no answers.

"What happens now?" Will whispered.

"Your guess is as good as mine," Levi replied.

They pushed as deep into the snow as they could. Their only chance to escape would come once the Blackfeet started their attack. Only then could they move unseen—if they were lucky and nobody got sight of them first.

The metallic click of a hammer—not theirs but somebody else's. Then a loud report and a puff of smoke came from the other side of the creek. Five seconds later, a cacophony of gunfire filled the air, leaving the opposite bank covered in gray-green smoke. Then the trappers began to return fire.

The mountain men were surprised that the Indians had so many guns. That was when they saw the Ute Indians at the stream's edge. There were two groups of Indians from different tribes, and the Blackfeet didn't know the Ute were watching them.

Sure, the Crow had some guns, too, but more were needed to go around. Only the chief and a few warriors had rifles, but most were reserved for the hunters. It was more important to feed hungry mouths than to use valuable black powder to kill White men when arrows usually did the trick. This wasn't the case with these Blackfeet on the warpath, though. They were armed to the teeth and loaded for bear.

"I wonder what's gonna happen now?" Levi whispered. "Things are lookin' worse every minute."

As the gunfire heightened, the occasional bullet slammed into the frozen creek bank, sending ice and dirt flying. The first couple of bullets were stray rounds. They were coming dangerously close to the mountain men in any case. Then the Ute warriors spotted them, and now they were in the open with little cover other than snow. Even their arrows would penetrate it enough to kill them, not to mention the chunks of lead from the flintlock long rifles of the Blackfeet.

Levi snapped a glance over his shoulder and yelled, "We've got to get out of here! I'm afraid we're gonna have to try to take sides with the White folks. If we don't, the Indians are gonna kill us."

A wild gleam shone in Forrester's eyes. He was a trained fighter and had fought with the army from the frontier forts and with Levi against the Comanche. The soldier in him emerged as bullets began to zing past their heads. He completely disregarded the danger. This was what he had been trained to do.

"And what if the trappers decide to shoot at us?" Will asked, apparently as cool and calm as a millpond despite the gunfire.

"If you have a better idea, I'm all ears, pard," Levi said as beads of sweat popped up on his brow and upper lip despite the cold. His eyes flashed all around him as he assessed the quickly changing situation.

They crawled out of the water as fast as they could. The rifles spitting bullets their way got them moving even quicker. They scurried up the slippery bank and ran holus-bolus for the trappers. The White men took cover behind trees and rocks around their camp while they returned fire. Levi and Will crouched and ran like the devil was after them toward their camp. When the trapper nearest them noticed motion from the corner of his eye, he swung his rifle toward Levi, who was in the lead.

"Don't shoot!" Levi screamed with his eyes stretched wide. "We're White folks just like you!"

As they ran into the White men's camp, Johnson couldn't help but notice the Indian woman tied hands and feet, but he tried to act like he didn't see her. Will glanced at his friend, but his face was a mask; still, Will saw the violence simmering just under the surface.

The surprise on the trapper's face was apparent. Johnson swung his rifle toward the attacking warrior braves and fired off a round right before Forrester followed suit. Since there was no time to exchange words, the trappers turned again and continued to fire to repel the war party. Now, seven rifles spat bullets back at the men across the broad stream.

The sun shined down, creating a glare, making it hard to spot the source of the incoming fire. The flash from barrels was the only hint. Gun smoke gave the men cover from both sides. They continued to fire blindly. Levi dove for cover as Forrester calmly returned fire with his four pistols as he stood in full view of his enemies. His long blond hair shined in the sunlight as he reloaded.

Levi yelled, "Get down, fool!" He grabbed Will's empty sleeve and dragged him to the ground and behind cover. "Whatcha tryin' to do? Get yourself shot?"

"I was intimidating the enemy and locating their positions to direct the return fire," Forrester replied. He almost sounded bored.

Levi looked at his friend like sometimes he didn't really know who it was living in there. He did some of the dangest things. He sure as heck wasn't afraid of anything anymore. Maybe he never was.

Just as suddenly as it began, the gunfire ceased. The silence seemed too quiet. Everybody knew something else was going to happen soon. They just didn't know what it would be. They lay there looking at each other, but nobody talked. Everybody was breathing like they had just run a marathon. The adrenaline was high, and hearts hammered in their chests. Every man there had his eyes spread wide. They all knew the warriors were still there. They doubted they planned to leave until they'd killed the White intruders.

Levi and Forrester were never caught out like they were this time. It was an unfortunate coincidence for the mountain men. It meant more guns for the trappers and thieves and more dead braves for the Blackfeet and Ute Indians. It was a question of how many men were they willing to lose before they turned and ran.

The White men were pinned down and couldn't move until nightfall, so they had no choice but to fight. If they ran, they would be cut down in their tracks. So far, the only reason they hadn't lost anybody was the fact that the Indians were such bad shots, and they took forever to reload their stolen rifles.

They must have recently acquired the long guns. None of the local White men sold too many rifles to the local Indians because they knew they could one day be used against them. Then again, this far west, some men would do anything for money, even if it meant endangering the lives of others. The mountain men believed the White trappers were driven by their greed.

As the breeze swept the gun smoke away, they had to be more careful when they stuck their heads up. They could see the outline of warrior braves between small clouds of gray smoke.

The trapper closest to Levi asked, "Where in the world did you fellas come from?"

Will went to answer, but Levi interrupted him and said, "We come from a compound a week down the mountain. My name is Levi Johnson, and this here's Captain Will Forrester."

He stopped Forrester from telling them they were trapping up there in the mountains, so they wouldn't suspect they were the owners of the beaver pelts they had stacked in a pile. They were frozen stiff and stolen, but now wasn't the time to confront five armed men who were already fighting a bunch of hostiles.

Now, they had to join forces or perish. Still, they

might perish just the same. That was when both Levi and Forrester noticed the black pieces of hair hanging from belts, necklaces, and saddles.

Two men hid behind two bales of scalps as they returned fire. On the ground near the fire were several bundles of freshly trapped pelts. The mountain men wondered when the scalpers would put the two together; they stole the furs from the two men who'd just stumbled into their camp to avoid hostile gunfire. The woman lay at the edge of their camp, moaning, half-conscious. Levi wondered who she was. She was dressed like a Crow Indian. He wondered if she had come from Hachta's camp.

"I'm Paul Dungun, that's Grover Greed, and these boys are Herman Horseshoe, Sandy Brush, and Steve Flint. We be trappers from over Kansas way."

"You're a long way off your graze, ain't cha?" Levi asked. He nodded toward the stack of beaver pelts. "It looks like you've had a good run."

"No more than most, I'd venture. I dare guess you ain't from around here as all the locals I seen be Indians," Paul said and almost grinned. Then he turned and fired another shot across the river. "My guess is we've got more black powder than the heathens over the creek."

"I don't know if you've noticed, but the Blackfeet and Ute warriors have us pinned down," Forrester huffed. "If we move, we're dead, even with the poor shots the Indians seem to be. There must be fifteen or twenty rifles over there. This isn't a turkey shoot because we can't even see them."

"And how are you so sure they're Ute and Blackfeet?" Paul asked suspiciously. "We can't tell one Indian tribe from another."

"Because that's my job as an Army captain," Will replied. "How would it look if I didn't know what tribes were active in the area?"

"You two don't look like much of an army," Herman observed.

"I've never seen Indians with so many weapons except Comanche," Levi said.

"You've seen real live Comanche Indians?" Hermon asked. He was so shocked that he forgot his last comment. "And you're still alive to talk about it?"

"We lost half our expedition to Comanche warriors," Forrester said. "I'm a captain in the army." He showed them his saber. "I'm mapping trails across the mountains. This is my scout. I'm not wearing my uniform because it's too danged cold."

"Whatcha doin' here in the dead of winter?" Paul asked.

"To find passable passages deeper into the Rockies," Forester lied. The last thing they wanted them to think was that they were trappers and the owners of the stolen pelts. It could cost them their lives. "We plan to map a new trail to California."

Levi glanced at his friend with a knowing look. "I've been tracking for the United States Army since way back in Kansas. I'm supposed to take the captain wherever he says."

"And how's it y'all only be two?" Paul asked. He appeared to the leader. A hint of suspicion crept into his voice.

"Why, I just told you," Forrester said as cold as ice.

"We ran into Comanche—twice. We're all that's left. The rest are all dead."

The statement sobered all five scalpers instantly. They all looked across the shallow water to where the Indians waited for them to stick their heads up so they could take another shot. They looked back at the two men dressed like the Indians shooting at them and decided they must know what they were talking about.

DAY ONE

(Two months earlier)

NONE OF THE SIX MOUNTAIN MEN THOUGHT MUCH OF making such a decision in the middle of winter. They were older and were more experienced with the dangerous blizzards that wreak havoc on the Rocky Mountains. But Levi Beaver Johnson wasn't afraid of the weather, and Forrester followed his friend wherever he went.

Levi thought he had found the perfect spot to trap beaver in the coldest months, when they had the heavy, dense coats from the cold water. But the local Indians had also ventured further into the wilderness to find fresh springs and creeks where beaver built their dams. When they located Beaver's discovery, they claimed it as their own because it was on their land.

The biggest problem was that they were Crow Indians, Rusty Steel's friends, especially Chief Hachta. They all realized that if the Indians claimed it was theirs, even though Levi had found it, it indeed belonged to them.

They had been there three thousand years, the White men only decades. Mountain Man Dennis believed the Crow had spotted Levi and Will going to trap the new streams and followed them to the secret spot. Now, it was no longer a secret.

When Dennis, Rusty, and Angus had started trapping in the Rockies, the Crow allocated an area for them to work in peace. The Indians, in turn, had somebody to trade with for steel tools and the occasional rifle. So, initially, it was a win-win situation. But that was before the beaver began to get trapped out in the nearby streams. Poachers were responsible for part of the decline in the population. White men were closing in from all sides, forging deeper into the wilderness in search of valuable pelts, even in dangerous places like the Rocky Mountains.

"I ain't one to tell folks what they should or shouldn't do, but you boys have never roughed it through a winter up here," Rusty huffed. "Out there some nights, you might find yourself in dire straits if the temperatures drop too low."

"I don't see how we have a choice," Levi replied. "Forrester and I are young and healthy and still have all our digits." He looked at his friend and added, "At least on the hands we got. I reckon it's too important not to try to find another spot before winter hits hard. If not, our season ain't gonna be what we thought back a month ago. As soon as the Crow claimed our streams, they shut us down. At least they let us keep our traps. They don't even know how to use my fish trap."

"I still don't like the idea of you two young fellas foresting through the mountains into the unknown," Rusty said. "There are places out there that Angus,

Dennis, and I ain't even seen. I imagine a danger or two we ain't experienced either. I've been told some places the Indians don't even go. There's said there was a point that you passed into a burial ground, and after that, it's full of demons. At least, that's what the Crow believe. Hachta claims that everybody that passed that point disappeared and was never seen again. That's why they figure there're bad spirits up there."

"If we wanna have good summer sales at the Rendezvous, we'll have to find some new springs and ponds to trap in," Levi huffed. "I don't dare return to the one I found. It belongs to Hachta and his hunters now. I figure we've got to find a place where nobody's gonna follow us. Then we'll trap until the weather gets too bad, and we'll come back to the compound. Hopefully, loaded down with pelts."

"We believe if the trapping is good, we can make a small lean-to as a shelter to keep the snow off and the warmth contained," Will said.

"The Crow Indians are still sort of touchy about that visit by your uncle, Will," Rusty said. "It's gonna take a spell for them to forget we brought 'im to their camp. The chief made it clear he didn't wanna see us for a spell. Lucky time heals, and they'll forget it as soon as something bigger pops up. Indians don't take much to the military because of their past aggressions and take less to an infamous major. You two will have to tread lightly out there. It's not just the weather that's dangerous. At least there shouldn't be many grizzlies anymore. Most of 'em will be in hibernation by now, although you might run into the odd one wanderin' until about mid-November."

"I've been caught out in blizzards back East," Levi

said. "I know a thing or two about surviving temperatures well below freezing. I realize Indiana ain't nothin' like the Rockies, but we ain't in January or February either. As far as the Indians go, I figure it's become the bread and butter of every day. Whatcha gonna do about it? Nothing I can see."

"If we were in January, there's no way I'd let you two go anywhere," Angus grumbled. "You'd have to go over my dead body. We've been through enough as it is. We don't need to go lookin' for trouble. In the Rockies, it comes and finds ya all on its own."

"In January, we'll all be inside the cabin curing the pelts y'all trap in the next few months," Dennis said. "Everything has its time and place, I reckon."

"Things get narrow and dodgy when you get deeper into the mountains," Rusty said. "The higher up you go, the worse the trail gets. You best take the mules and walk, because the horses ain't surefooted enough. They'll never make it where you wanna go."

"We'll load up Dot with supplies, and we can take Bessy to carry the rest of the traps," Levi said. "If that's all right with you, Rusty."

"I was gonna suggest you take her," the aging mountain man replied as he stroked his long gray beard. "She's as surefooted as they come, and she never gets tired, although she may get stubborn if she's pressed. If you find a spot, you'll have to build a shelter for the mules too. You don't want 'em freezin' to death. Then you'll be comin' back empty-handed."

"I'll get to it right now," Will said.

Forrester seemed eager to go someplace—any place would do. He had suffered the presence of his uncle and now wanted to get as far away as possible for a spell. Of course, he knew Major Warren Forrester was long dead and buried, but even his spirit was still evil. His nephew didn't even want to know where the grave was.

The man was so wicked that Will feared the devil would be near wherever he was buried. Even though he had never been a superstitious man, something he'd seen in his uncle's eyes made him doubt everything. The last thing he expected was to find his family breathing and breeding pure death and destruction.

Ex-Captain Will Forrester grabbed his grizzly bear coat, slipped it over his stump, pushed his left arm through, and pulled it tight. The temperatures had dropped in the last weeks, and now it was near freezing. The coat's right sleeve was folded and sewn closed to keep the weather out. Despite the loss of his arm, Will took the challenge head-on and never mentioned his missing limb. He pulled his raccoon skin hat tight.

It was still early. The sun had come up an hour before. When Will stepped outside, his breath showed in the frigid air. The cold wind hit him in the face like an unexpected slap. The snow shined like millions of diamonds and crushed under his feet. The sun rose over the jagged mountains. The winter rope ran from the front door to the outhouse and the stables. The other two cabins were also connected with rope, so if a blizzard blew up and they had a white-out, they could find their way like blind men.

Meanwhile, Levi prepared the traps and a supply of food for a month. They didn't know how long they would be out—they would search as long as it took. He had become the most resourceful hunter of the eight mountain men who lived on the mountain. He wasn't worried about food. It was the unknown that concerned him. They were headed into the wilderness farther than Dennis, Angus, or even Rusty had penetrated. Nobody knew what was beyond, but the two young mountain men were just about to go and find out. Dennis had returned to his cabin, and Rusty and Angus helped Levi pack their supplies on the mules. They brayed and groaned under the weight even though the mountain men never overloaded the animals.

An hour later, they had their snowshoes on and were trekking toward the north path out the other end of the compound. Trails of smoke could be seen spiraling out the chimneys. The cold had arrived, and it would only be getting worse. But still, there was enough time before they got snowed in somewhere up there, higher into the mountains.

Even the mules' breaths were seen in the cold morning. Will's nose was already red, but neither he nor Levi minded. They had seen worse cold snaps back East.

The only noise was the crushing ice under the animals' feet and hooves. There wasn't anything living in sight, but Levi knew they were there: the wild animals and maybe even Indians. They had followed him to their last beaver stream and pond, so he had to make sure they couldn't find this one. He would have to follow up to make sure no Crow, Blackfoot, or Ute spies were watching where they went.

On this trip, the ex-army captain decided to use his education and began mapping out the trails through the Rocky Mountains. He had already made maps of their compound and the surrounding areas and all the way down the mountain to where the Rendezvous was held last year. Of course, he omitted the presence of the large Crow camp in case it fell into the wrong hands and was seen by the wrong eyes. He planned to map their journey as they plunged into the unknown.

Piles of snow sat perched on the pine needle-filled limbs. Four-foot-deep snowdrifts piled on the leeward side of the massive trees. They swayed back and forth in the icy breeze as it whistled in the pines. Occasionally, a gust of wind came up, and clumps of snow fell to earth. One fell on Forrester's back. The raccoon skin cap protected his head, but a clump of snow worked its way down his neck and sent cold chills up his spine.

As Rusty and Angus watched, the two men became smaller and smaller until they disappeared into the tree line. Both men wore concerned looks. They knew how treacherous the Rockies were, and even they didn't know the dangers that lurked beyond where they had ventured. But Levi had decided to push the outside of the envelope and dare to step where no man had dared, and his friend Will Forrester was his willing accomplice.

DAY TWO

THE FIRST NIGHT, THEY SLEPT IN A CAVE LEVI HAD discovered on his previous ventures into the wilderness looking for new spots to hunt wild game, especially to trap beaver. It would take a few days to get to country that none of the older mountain men had explored. Levi and Will were looking for uncharted lands where even Indians hadn't gone—if such a place existed. They had no idea what awaited them past the part of the wilderness they had traveled so often. Now, they were setting a new course.

"Do you think there are any bears in this cave?" Forrester asked, wide-eyed. "I'd hate to wake one up from their hibernation. I've encountered enough bears for a lifetime."

"I know the cave's deep, but I never ventured farther than the mouth to check." Levi chuckled. "I know it's full of bats. There may be a bear in there sleeping the winter, but I doubt we wake 'im. As long as we don't shoot off our guns, I doubt we stir anything up."

"I'm gonna have to sleep with one eye open anyway,"

Will replied. "I have an inherent fear of grizzly bears after my last dance with one. I don't know which one I fear most, the grizzlies or the Comanche."

"Everybody's scared of grizzlies, pard." Levi smiled. "Only a fool ain't frightened of the most dangerous animal in the wilderness, apart from man. Not to mention Comanche. I doubt we run into any so far off their hunting grounds, but you just never know. They move around like no other tribe. I've heard of 'em ridin' hundreds of miles to strike. Apparently, they ain't got the words 'too far' in their vocabulary."

Levi was totally relaxed despite the possibility of a bear living where they planned to spend the night. Forrester was the opposite side of the coin. Johnson slept like he didn't have a care in the world. Despite the lack of concern from Levi, Will still felt like the bear would appear sometime during the night when he was asleep. So, he spent a sleepless night while Levi snored and slept like a baby. The ex-captain lay with his gun in his lap the whole evening.

Will Forrester wasn't usually nervous and seldom let Mr. Paranoia perch on his shoulder. But his fear of bears was somehow different. He didn't even flinch when attacked by Indian warriors, who scared the hell out of Levi. Everybody had something they were scared of— unless they were a psychopath.

All through the night, Will fed wood to the fire. The flames warmed the two men as they cast dancing shadows on the cave's walls. The breeze blew the cinders toward the ceiling and deeper into the cave. Forrester assumed there was more than one entrance. Smoke hung a foot from the ceiling before it was sucked into the depths of the dark cavern.

Forrester strained to hear, mistaking the sounds of mice, rats, and bats for grizzly bears. He could hear his heart pounding between his ears. He lay with his eyes staring into the black hole before him. From the cave's opening, stars appeared like they spilled from a bucket. Clouds passed between the earth and the little moon available. The winter winds blew through the night, bringing occasional snow flurries. By morning, their footprints from the day before were gone.

Outside the cave, on the ledge of the trail up the mountain, the mules dug their hooves at the snow, trying to uncover some grass. They slid their jaws as their breaths showed in the frigid morning air.

By the time Levi awoke, Will was busy making breakfast. Thick strips of salted bacon hung over a steel bar by the fire. Orange coals heated the pork as falling grease sizzled. It glowed on Will's face as Levi yawned into a stretch. He sat up and pulled on his boots.

"How about some of that coffee?" Levi asked. "You look like you ain't slept a wink."

Johnson stood slipping his brace of pistols into his belt.

"I didn't," Will replied, too tired to smile. After a full day of trekking up the steep part of the mountains, he was out of energy without the night's sleep.

"You're movin' around like a sloth." Levi laughed. "I ain't ever seen ya so slow."

"You'd be slow too if you couldn't sleep after yesterday's climb," Will snapped. He was still on edge, and the lack of sleep left him edgier and grumpy.

Levi looked at his friend questioningly. He understood his fear of bears because he had danced with a couple, too, so it wasn't something to laugh at.

Bugs crawled across the floor, and spider webs stretched across the ceiling and every crook and cranny of the cave. Small four-legged animals scurried in the dark.

"I think you best slow down a bit, pilgrim," Levi said. "We ain't seen a single sign of bear, have we? And here you're as nervous as a dog with ticks."

"No, I guess not," Will said as his blue eyes peeked over the brim of his tin coffee cup. "If I think about it logically, I know I'm wrong. But I've found in the past that logic doesn't work very well in the wilderness, so my faith in normality wavers. We usually get caught off guard by most situations, as they come unexpectedly. I waited for the bear to come all night, convinced he was there. To be honest, I haven't heard anything but bats and mice. Still, I have a gut feeling that's chewing at my stomach, and I can't seem to shake it."

"If it's your gut feelin', then it's a whole different matter." Levi laughed. "I've gotta gut too, and all it's sayin' is that it's hungry. Now, if you don't mind puttin' the grizzly bear nonsense aside and finish breakfast, we might get out of here by noon."

Levi pulled on his fur coat and walked outside to relieve himself. The cold breeze felt good, slapping him in the face. It woke him up instantly. Everything was white as far as the eye could see. He looked over the ledge along the trail and spat. He counted as it fell. It looked like a reasonable drop down the side.

Beaver didn't think many hunters, or even Indians, would venture too far into the Rockies in the winter. He knew they had just started, but he had forgotten how difficult it was, and it was going to get much more so shortly.

Will walked up beside his friend and gave him a hot cup of coffee. Steam rose from the surface. They stood in comfortable silence, looking at the wonder of nature, the Rocky Mountains. They awoke to the same views every day, but each day was like it was the first time. It was breathtaking. The sun's first rays shot into the sky on the jagged eastern horizon, and a prism of colors followed.

Will nodded forward and slapped his neck. It felt like a bug was crawling down his coat. Immediately after, he felt a faint breeze blow the back of his hair. He closed his eyes and listened to the wind—he thought he heard something else out there. He took a breath, but the wind took any smells away. His face stung as the gusts peppered his cheeks.

They stood at the edge of the drop-off of some fifty feet and watched the morning come and the stars vanish on the other side of the world. They squinted their eyes against the crystal-like surface of snow glowing in the sunlight.

Three shadows stood long beside them as the sun rose in the sky like it hung from a string. One towered over the other two. Will was the first to notice the extra shadow. That was about the same time he felt the hot breath on the back of his neck. He shot a glance over his shoulder, and the bear roared in his face. He smelled its rancid breath as it emptied its lungs in an earth-shattering clamor.

It frightened Forrester so much that he leaped forward. Will dropped off the cliff like a rock. As he fell, he crashed through limbs and vegetation protruding from the stone wall. It broke his fall. He looked up at Levi as he stared down at him, puzzled. He moved faster than the bear and pulled both pistols from his belt. The massive bear swatted at the first bullet like a pesky fly.

The second bullet exploded its eye. The roar became a high-pitched cry as the animal clawed at its face. Levi didn't waste a second as he dove for the cave, rolling on the ground out of reach of the angry bear. He pulled back the hammer on his rifle as he swung the barrel and shot out the grizzly's other eye.

It continued to roar. Neither bullet made an exit wound, so the shots weren't deadly. Levi dove for cover, but even though the bear was blind, it could smell and hear him just fine. He lunged in the direction of the human. Johnson dodged yet another advance from the grizzly as he rolled precariously back toward the cliff.

"Come and get me, you hairy beast!" Levi roared.

The bear turned and swatted its giant paws in the air. The young mountain man grabbed a loose stone from the ground and threw it at the grizzly, hitting him square in the snout. It roared toward the projectile's origin, but Levi wasn't there. He had dropped over the ledge and hung on with his fingers as the grizzly rushed out into space. Its limbs flailed when it felt the ground disappear from under it. It fell like a ton of bricks and crashed at the bottom, not five feet from where Forrester landed.

He had been watching the whole thing from his back on the ground, but when he saw Levi struggle with the man-killer, he scrambled to his feet and tried to scale the cliff. He watched as the furry body dropped right past his face. His eyes locked with the bear's empty sockets for a fraction of a second.

It hit the ground with a massive thud as puffs of fresh snow billowed around it. The bear took a dozen ragged breaths before it sighed for the last time. A foot twitched a few times, then it died. Will was halfway up the cliff, hanging onto a root for dear life. His eyes were bugging out of his head. He looked up and saw Levi hanging by his fingers.

Johnson looked down—it made him dizzy. He saw the bear motionless and Will between him and the dead animal. He couldn't help but crack a little smile. He even chuckled. He'd never been in this situation before, and he was sure his buddy, Forrester, hadn't either. He pulled himself up, got an elbow on the ledge, hauled his body over the top, and rolled to safety. His lungs sounded like a steam engine as he huffed and gulped for air.

"That was as close as it gets," Levi whispered.

He thought he heard more sounds from somewhere past the curtain of darkness deeper into the cavern where the bear lived. Was there a second grizzly in there? Johnson stood spellbound as his friend clawed his way to the top and pulled himself over the ledge.

"What is it now?" Forrester asked as he stared into the dark cavern, gasping for oxygen. His brow furrowed, and his face glistened with sweat. "It can't be another bear, can it?"

"I could swear I heard somethin' else back in that cave," Levi said as he reloaded his rifle. "I ain't never seen two bears in the same cave, but just because I ain't seen it don't mean it can't happen, now does it?"

When it came, both men dove for the ground and buried their faces in the dirt. In their escape, the mountain men could feel them touch their bodies. A black cloud flew into the cavern. The mass of bats seemed to take forever to all enter their home. They came by the hundreds, if not by the thousands. Bugs scurried over the mountain men's heads and under their bodies as they ran for cover from the flying mammals.

Finally, they returned to the darkness. The colony's last hundred or so strays flew deep inside and disappeared silently over their heads. Shivers ran up and down the mountain men's spines. Levi turned his head toward Will, and they exchanged looks.

"Was that crazy or what?" Levi asked, smiling. "And we ain't even eaten breakfast yet. What else is gonna happen today?"

"Anything," Will replied, still dazed by what they had witnessed. "From now on, I don't rule out anything at all. No matter what we do, the wilderness throws a wrench in the works and catches us off guard."

"No, sir, this time you had it right, and my lackadaisical nature got in the way, and I didn't listen to you. Your gut feeling was spot-on," Levi said.

Will Forrester smiled at the acknowledgment. He knew his buddy was much more of a mountain man than he was, but he was glad he seemed to be learning too. Maybe slower than Beaver Johnson, but still, he needed to improve.

"If we keep it up, one of these times, we may not win the day," Will huffed, even though he was chaffed by what Levi had said.

"Like I always say, iffin you don't expect nothin', you'll never be disappointed." Levi smiled.

"That's something that's going to take me time to learn," Will replied. "My emotions get in my way when things get chaotic, but only with grizzly bears. Fortunately, I don't suffer the same with Indians."

"We better get back down there with the mules and skin that bear," Levi said.

Forrester looked over the cliff and down the way he had just come up. "There's plenty of meat on those bones. Especially as it was about to go into hibernation, and we can always use another skin."

"First, we've gotta run the mules down," Levi said as he looked down the trail. "They would have to go in the wrong direction."

The Journey

"We best eat despite the scare," Levi said. "We're gonna need all the energy we can get for the trek ahead of us. We can't start wearin' down already. We've gotta step up our pace, or we're not gonna get anywhere."

"I'm all right," Forrester said. "The bacon and coffee will give me enough energy. Don't worry about me. I'll keep up just like I always do."

The young mountain men broke open the biscuits, slapped some bacon in between, and ate four each. Then they drank the rest of the coffee. They pulled some hard tack for later and stuffed some biscuits into their pockets for lunch. They didn't have time to linger. They not only had to find a new place to trap, but they also had to catch enough beaver to load the mules as much as they could. And they had only two months to do it. That included making a provisional lean-to as well.

Levi smiled at his friend and said, "This ain't a competition, ya know. You don't have to take everything so seriously. Today is just another day, brother. Let's go see what else is waitin' on us."

"That's just what I'm afraid of," Will replied. "What's waiting on us."

It looked like it would take a lot of time. Of course, it all depended on how far they had to travel in such conditions before they found a pristine stretch of land. It would require plenty of springs and ponds where beavers had built their dams. They still needed to learn how long that would take, too.

By the time they rounded up the mules, which had run down the mountain as soon as they got a whiff of the grizzly bear, it was late. The path was only wide enough for one animal to climb at a time.

As they climbed over the peaks to reach the distant valleys, the air grew thin, and the cold deepened. They had to lean into the gusts of wind on the slopes, then they would drop into a valley, and the wind would disappear, and the sun warmed their faces despite the temperatures. Some valleys stretched for miles and miles. They searched for lines of thicker vegetation, for any indication of where a stream might run, or a small river might be—a place without too much current for the sturdy beaver to make dams.

Levi envisioned a bonanza of beaver somewhere in front of them. He had found the last place, and it was close to the cabins but challenging to locate. Johnson used the lay and structure of the land to look for running water, and when he found that, they would search for dams and holes in the ice. He wasn't only an expert tracker and trapper; he also knew how to use the lay of the land for what he sought. Now, he looked for lines of trees along a frozen stream.

Johnson led the way with Dot in tow as Will held the lead of Bessy, Rusty Steel's mule. She was aging like her owner but was still as faithful as an old dog. One moment the trail was narrow and slippery, and the next, it opened into valleys they had to cross. They were constantly aware when they were in the open and tried not to make silhouettes on the horizon. As far as they could see, there wasn't another living soul in sight, but they knew first impressions in the wilderness could be deceiving.

Even though they couldn't see them, there could be any number of Indians hiding anywhere around them. Maybe even buried in the snow. Rusty Steel had told them about ambushes that played out just like that, and they butchered their enemies through the element of surprise. So, Levi carefully inspected the surface of the snow before them, ensuring it was untouched by humans.

The valleys were covered in deeper snow, making the mules struggle as the men walked on top of the soft powder with snowshoes. They left a track like a slug across the frigid mountains. The sun shined so brightly they had to squint to continue across the stretches of flat land. Then they began to climb yet another steep path and up another pass only to arrive at the top and stop. It was so abrupt that Will walked into the back of Dot.

"What the—?" Forrester asked.

Levi held his hand up as they pulled the animals to a halt. They both looked and listened. They locked stretched eyes with raised eyebrows. The blood drained from Levi's face. He didn't like what he saw in front of them.

"I don't know if I dare walk through there with the

mules and all," Levi said. "I know for a fact that Indians don't take to folks from other tribes trepassin' on their burial grounds. It's even worse for a White man to set foot inside. I heard Rusty tell me stories of just such a situation that riled the Indians to no end."

"But they're only dead men and women," Will said. "It's not like we've never seen a dead Indian or White man, for that matter. Since leaving Kansas, we've left a trail of dead bodies, Indians and soldiers. It's a miracle we haven't been included."

An eerie silence fell over the party. Their words sounded like they came from a bullhorn but were only whispers. The glowing sun was clouded over, darkening everything. Both young mountain men thought they saw things where there was nothing. The clouds cast shadows on the land and mountains as they traveled quickly past overhead.

The vision before them was strange, even for an above-ground cemetery. The smell of fowl and the sound of flapping wings filled the air.

"There must be three hundred crows sittin' perched on the burial platforms," Levi whispered. Neither man dared speak loudly. "I've never seen so many crows in one place."

Suddenly, hoarse-sounding croaks came from the birds—hundreds of them. The racket was so annoying that the mules startled and kicked and tried to buck their loads off their backs.

"Them ain't crows," Levi whispered. "They're ravens. The sign of death in Southeastern Indiana, where I'm from."

"That's old folklore," Will replied, as he chuckled. "You aren't superstitious, are you, Levi?"

"Why, no more than most folks, I reckon," Johnson answered, but the concern showed on his face. "Then again, we ain't in Kansas anymore, pilgrim."

"What do you propose we do, partner?" Will asked. He still had a smile on his lips.

Levi pulled on his full beard as he weighed the pros and cons of trespassing on Indian burial grounds. He was obviously not convinced like Forrester was. He had his doubts as to proceeding. He looked carefully around them. He had to try to figure out how he would go around if he could, but it looked like they couldn't unless they walked back a day and took another pass to the other side of the mountain.

"We don't even know what tribe the cemetery belongs to," Will yelled over the caws of the ravens. Like most well-educated men, he didn't have an ounce of superstition in him. He chuckled at the puzzled look on his friend's face.

"I can't see losing two days by backtrackin'," Levi huffed. "I reckon you're right. It's just a stupid superstition, anyway."

The birds suddenly became silent as soon as they stepped into the burial ground. It was instant and absolute. It gave both men an eerie feeling despite their beliefs. Any man in his right mind would be scared walking through such a place. Dead bodies and, in many places, skeletons lay on beds suspended off the ground by long poles. Blackbirds perched on every platform available.

The Indians believed that if the birds ate their remains, they would fly away with the spirits. Again, the ravens and crows began with their noisy banter. They all accusingly pointed their beaks at the intruders and cawed. The ravens sounded deeper than the crows, but they were all nerve-racking. Black wings flapped on every burial tree. Some were wrapped in colorful blankets and rested in the cradle of three-pronged trees. Others were tied to protruding limbs.

Some system of the caste was obvious. The chiefs and medicine men lay in the four-posted platforms with their bodies and personal possessions beside them. The older ones were apparent because the cloth had rotted and fallen away from the skeletons.

Will pulled a pistol, held it up, and fired—a loud crack followed by a flame and puff of smoke. Feathers flew through the air as hundreds of birds took flight simultaneously. The sound of flapping wings replaced the crowing. A black cloud of crows and ravens blotted out the sun momentarily, making the place even scarier for the intruders. Even Forrester was a little shaken.

"Come on," Levi huffed as they began to move forward. They had to coax and pull the mules to get them to continue up the trail, which ran right through the burial ground. The only path winded around and back again, making them walk past hundreds of burial trees and platforms. There were many more there than they had initially thought. It stretched half the width of the little valley.

"Why in the world would Indians bring their dead to such a faraway place?" Levi asked. "It must be some special place for there to be so many bodies. I wonder if they be Ute or Blackfeet. Maybe even Crow."

"This looks like decades of dead," Will whispered. "Some of the bones look like clay or dust."

Now, the only sounds were the soft hooves of the mules and the occasional blowing of Bessy. She, like her owner, didn't like Indian burial grounds. Levi didn't either. He wondered how they could return and not cross back in the same way. Will examined the dead like he was studying a course back at West Point. He even took out a notepad he used to map their travels. He made small drawings of the shape of the mountain peaks that towered over them.

Levi tried to ignore so many dead bodies everywhere he looked. It made him nervous being in the middle of hundreds of open graves. He wasn't educated, although he could read, unlike his father. His mother home-schooled him and did a fine job, but it couldn't be compared to the ex-army captain's education. He was a West Point graduate. It was sometimes hard to figure out who was teaching whom, however. The value of a college education seemed pointless in the wilderness, but Forrester's brains had gotten them out of a jam on more than one occasion.

The trail through the mass of graves seemed to be endless. Then again, it could be that it seemed endless due to the nature of their environment. It would make a ghost jumpy.

Despite the cold and the snow, a blanket of fog seemed to hover a few inches over the ground. It made both men even more nervous. They could hardly tell where they stepped a foot. Little by little, the crows and ravens returned and began to caw again. It was like they were yelling for the White men to leave their place in peace. They felt all the more like trespassers. When they finally saw the other side of the graveyard, it seemed forever to reach it.

The path continued to curl around, eventually leaving them on the other side. Here a shrine had been built. It arched the entrance to the burial grounds and was decorated with human bones. Shin bones, thigh bones, and even ribs hung from what looked like the entrance. It appeared they had come in through the exit.

Beside the shrine was a sepulcher. Inside were several skulls decorated with beads and scalps. Snow covered everything in sight except the recess with the dead men's heads.

"This is one scary place," Levi huffed. "I ain't ever seen nothin' like it."

"If this is the entrance, what awaits us down the trail?" Forrester asked as his eyes narrowed while looking into the distance.

"I'd hate even to guess," Levi whispered.

They had left the noise of the ravens and crows behind, but they couldn't shake what they had just seen.

"I've seen my share of cemeteries," Will said, "but I've never seen anything like that. I dread going back through."

"But you said they were just dead men and women, didn't ya?" Levi replied. "I told ya it wasn't a good idea to trespass. Now, I reckon we're gonna pay for our ways. I wish I'd have followed my gut feelin' even if it did cost us two days. In the end, if we run into trouble, it'll cost us more anyway."

Even the mules were hurrying to get as far away from the burial ground as fast as they could. Bessy amazed both men and broke into a trot. Levi shot a glance over his shoulder, and a shiver ran up his spine. He was going to have to find another way back down the mountain. He doubted they would be lucky twice—if they were really lucky at all. Maybe it was too late already.

Vultures circled overhead in the frigid air. They could still see flocks of crows come and go. The chatter slowly disappeared as they gained more distance. Even Levi and Forrester found themselves nearly trotting to get away. In the back of Johnson's mind, visions of what might be in store for them were pushed into the dark corners. He forced himself to focus and shake off the bad feeling they got from crossing the path of the dead.

The day started to wane, and the sun neared the nearest mountain. As they climbed into the shadows, the cold deepened. Both men wore appropriate coats, moccasins, and fur caps to keep them warm. It would have to get a lot colder for Levi Johnson to slow down.

Deep inside, he knew he chose to venture into the winter to hunt for more beaver because he wanted to prove himself. He still had to figure out to whom he was proving himself.

RUSTY STEEL

"Dagnabit, I knew I shouldn't have let those two young fellas run off to do such a difficult task," Rusty grumbled. "It's dangerous enough trappin' around here of a winter. I'd hate to see somethin' happen to 'em. They's good boys—even Will."

"Yeah, I reckon he's gone and proved himself fine and dandy-like." Angus grinned. "Despite the loss of his right arm. He's made one heck of a change from a fancy soldier to a frontiersman and a pioneer."

Angus sucked on his quid and spat into a peach can. Rusty puffed on a ceramic pipe as smoke billowed around his head. A jug of corn liquor sat in the middle of the table to spike the coffee and take off the chill after visiting the outhouse. Originally, they just went to the woods, but back when the Indians were more hostile, they built an outhouse at the edge of the compound. It was common practice for Indians to sneak up on enemies while doing their business and catch them off guard. But it's much more difficult to shoot a man with an arrow when he's sitting in a wooden building.

"Why, I figure that's what made him turn his life around and become more of a man." Rusty chuckled. "Sure, he was a sight to see in his uniform and on that white stallion of his, but it wasn't meant for 'im, even if his folks thought it was. Remember what it did to Major Warren Forrester, his uncle. Livin' such a life can do that to a man—maybe not all but a few."

"I wonder what the Crow did with the major?" Angus asked as he stared out the window. He blinked as the bright sun reflected off the fresh coat of snow. He pulled a tobacco twist from his pocket and bit off a fresh quid.

"Oh, I reckon they gave him what he deserved." Rusty snickered. "Hachta probably turned 'im over to the old women to torture. There's a couple of 'em that can take a man's life so slowly he don't even know when he crossed into the dark. Some of the Crow medicine men say one of them old girls can torture 'em after they're dead. I figure his head is stuck on a post somewhere at the edge of their camp right about now. There's no way he's still alive. The sooner he's gone, the sooner he'll be forgotten."

"I hope Hachta forgives us for bringing that major up there," Angus said. "It was a fool thing to do. We should have known better. It's just with him bein' Will's uncle and all, I never imagined he was such a wicked fella."

"Hindsight is a bugger, ain't it?" Rusty laughed. "Hachta had to save face and show he's the boss—that's all. That's why he ran us off like he did. That, and to keep his warriors from making a blunder we'd all regret. A chief don't have all that much control of his braves when things get heated up like then. Indian laws are a little looser than White man's laws.

"He'll come around once the winter passes, and he and his tribe need new steel tools, black powder, tobacco, and coffee. Once ya have 'em, you can't live without 'em even if they are the basic essentials. We always got a stock just for such an occasion. Just enough to keep 'em happy. Maybe once a year, a rifle. It's a small price to have this part of the mountain for ourselves."

"Essentials—that's a big word," Angus said. "E-ssentials. It sounds pretty and all."

Snowflakes as big as silver eagles floated down from the heavens. The air had vanished, at least near the cabins. Higher up was another matter. Rusty looked out the window beside Angus as they sipped hot cups of coffee. The aroma floated through the air. Rusty stared at the trail leading out of the compound and higher. He wondered how far the boys would try to climb to find a hidden valley on the other side.

Rusty Steel had seen more of the Rocky Mountains than even Dennis Breed. But he knew Levi had it in him to try to outdo them all. He had proved himself a better trapper than them and even designed his own for every sort of fish and small animal. He was probably a better shot than Rusty by now, too—especially with his new rifle. Now, he wanted to venture farther than any of them.

"I wonder what drives that boy so," Rusty said. "It's rare to see a young fella with so much gumption."

"You mean Levi?" Angus asked. "Why, I reckon he's one of a kind."

"One of a kind, ya say?" Rusty replied. He hesitated

as he pondered. "It could be. I reckon right about now, he's bein' put to the test. I figure soon we'll all find out what he's really made of."

"Even more important, he'll find out what he's really made of," Angus said. "It don't matter what we think. It's him that has to convince himself. I figure that's what he's really doin'. Havin' a look-see to find out who he is and what his limitations are. That's another one of them big words. Limitations. It sounds nice too."

"A man can't really find out how far he can go until he tries to go too far," Rusty said as he thought. "Then, if he's lucky enough to survive, he'll know exactly who he is and what he can and can't do."

"If that's his plan, I hope the captain can hold on to his hat 'cause that's gonna be one wild ride," Angus huffed.

The large fireplace roared behind the aging mountain men. Waves of heat warmed their backs as they sipped at hot beverages in tin cups, daydreamed, and stared out the window. They remembered how they felt when they were Levi's age. They understood exactly how he felt. They hadn't followed similar paths, but just the same, they understood. Rusty had lived several very different lives and wondered if this was his last change. He hadn't ever had any control over the other changes in his life, so he didn't expect the future to be any different.

As far as Rusty could see, most people had little control over their lives. Trouble and change seemed to pop up at the most unexpected moments. A man never knew what he would wake up to in the wilderness. Some days were good and some not so much, but each and every one was full of life and nature—and sometimes death.

Rusty Steel started life as a river-rat orphan and thief. He had the good fortune to be saved from the dregs of St. Louis and made a sailor, eventually becoming a captain despite his beginning. Later, things changed again, and all he had earned was lost. Then he took on yet another life and lived with the Crow Indians. Finally, he arrived where he now lived, perhaps during his final years. He was still ten years younger than Angus and had some fire left in him. Rusty could still smell the wood burning inside.

"Do you ever think about movin' back to civilization?" Rusty asked. He looked at Angus.

"Why, I haven't even thought about it for neigh on five or six years at least. That was probably the last time you brought it up. I used to, though. I even fancied it for a time. It takes some gettin' used to, livin' up here alone. But now, I figure I'm so used to peace and quiet I can't see a change."

"What I've observed about life is that I never have any control when the time for change comes," Rusty said. "It always comes along all on its lonesome and all sudden-like. Usually after death and disaster."

"Why, ain't you full of sunshine and roses today?" Angus chuckled. He was used to Rusty's nature.

Rusty gave him a dirty look and turned his eyes back to the mountains that towered over the compound. Outside, the temperatures were dropping a little more every few days.

"I sort of envy 'em," Angus said. "I used to be like that, and when I first met you, you were too."

"I don't envy anybody, ever," Rusty growled.

"Ain'tcha glad ya got all that fuss and busy out of ya?" Angus asked. "We ain't so reckless anymore, pard. We've learned to relax and enjoy life. It beats the dickens out of living in a cage in some tall building in a big city. Most city folks live in roosts like in a chicken house, all on top of each other. Why, I wouldn't be able to breathe."

"I ain't seen a big city since St. Louis," Rusty said. "Even then, I lived on my boat. I wasn't such a land lover back then. I'd have never imagined I'd end up where I did."

"From my observation, most folks that come to the mountains are runnin' from somethin' much like you were, and Forrester too," Angus said. "Only Dennis, Levi, and I came here because we wanted to. Not that it makes any difference. Most folks that come to live up here can't hack it anyway. So, after their first winter, they mosey back to where they came from."

"That is a fact," Rusty agreed, still worried. "I have half a mind to follow those two just to make sure they don't run into something they don't know how to get out of. I hope Levi ain't bit off more than he can chew."

"Levi Johnson can take care of himself just as good as you can, pilgrim," Angus said. "And he can take care of Will, too. Why don't you relax and enjoy the fact we've got those two young, strong men to do our jobs?" Angus cackled like a jackal.

They passed their days looking out the window as they worked fur and hides. There was never an idle moment even though all the hard work for the winter had been done. Levi had chopped enough wood for all three cabins. He chopped trees up like most people broke up toothpicks.

Rusty and Angus met daily with Dennis, Sam, Pete, and Bob. Often, they sat in Angus's cabin and worked the hides as they told tales, exaggerations, and a few white lies.

Black smoke squirreled out of all three chimneys. The blizzard ropes still connected the cabins. Icicles hung in the breeze from the hemp rope as it swung in the winter wind. There were footpaths between the buildings and the double outhouse. Snowdrifts piled against the zig-zag fence as the horses ran around the stables.

The sun glared down, making for a warmer fall than usual. A flock of crows flew over the cabin, nearly blocking out the light. It happened right before Angus and Rusty's eyes. Steel rushed to the door and opened it. The cold hit him like a punch in the face.

"We're on an endless ride of anything can happen," Rusty said as he looked at the sky. It was covered in blackbirds, both crows and ravens. "I ain't never seen nothin' like that."

Angus pushed Rusty aside and turned his face to the sky. "It looks like somethin' out of the Bible," McFarlin whispered.

"What part's that?" Rusty asked. The cloud of birds passed, and the sun returned.

"The part where God gets real danged mad," Angus whispered.

"And why would God be mad with us?" Rusty said. "We ain't don't nothin'."

"Maybe he ain't mad at us," Angus replied in a whisper. "But whoever it is got him angry, I wanna stay as far away as I can. We've had enough excitement for one winter with Forrester's uncle."

"Ain't that the truth," Rusty replied.

"Young or old, they always seem to get into trouble when they get to the Rocky Mountains," Angus said.

"You can pert near count on it," Rusty said. "I always say just pay your bills and don't kill anybody, and everything will be all right."

"I have a notion I'm gonna be around for a long time," Angus said, "and ya can't change a notion."

"I reckon everything starts dyin' as soon as it's born," Rusty said as he looked at Angus. "Sometimes, it's short, like Major Warren Forrester, and sometimes, it's long, like yours, Angus. Why, you might still be around long after me and maybe even the boys."

"Here, I thought I made a new friend, and it was only a shadow." Angus chuckled. "Iffin everybody around ya dies, what's the use of livin'?"

"From the first moment I met that major, I didn't trust him. Not even if I'd have met him in a prayer meetin'."

"Why didn't I hear ya say nothin' about it before we took 'im to the Crow camp then?" Angus asked. "You got drawn in hook, line, and sinker just like the rest of us did, you old fool. You make me so mad I could smoke a pickle."

"Me?" Rusty retorted. "You're the only man I know that can put both your feet in his mouth at the same time."

"And who's been pushin' your swing, mister know-it-all?" Angus asked. "Ever since Levi and Forrester left, you've been actin' like a grasshopper on loco weed. Iffin you're gonna keep pesterin' me, go ahead and go."

Rusty huffed, stood, and threw a log on the fire. The

reflection of the flames danced in his eyes, but his brow was furrowed, and concern covered his face.

"Don't worry so much, pard," Angus said. "It ain't healthy to fret. Levi is harder than a coffin nail. Since Will is with 'im, they'll be as safe as a tick on a hound dog with a stiff neck."

PARADISE

It took them two arduous weeks to arrive at what Levi considered the appropriate ground formations and vegetation growth. Luckily, the weather hadn't deteriorated. It had gotten a little warmer. In some places, the snow had turned into sludge and mud. There was virtually no trail to be seen. Johnson had been using the lay of the land to lead him where he wanted to go. They had run totally off their known grid and were in uncharted waters.

"Rusty Steel told me when you get a spell of good weather in the Rocky Mountains of a fall, you best get ready 'cause some real bad weather is gonna fall," Levi said as he held the flat of his hand over his eyes to block out the reflection of the crystal-covered snow. He pulled off his raccoon skin cap and wiped his brow with the sleeve of his bearskin coat. "I figure right over there is where we're gonna find those streams we're lookin' for. I found the last one in the summer, so it was easier to locate. There was more vegetation, and I could hear the running water. Here, it's provin' to be a bit more challengin'."

"Do you really think it's going to be any different today?" Will asked. "You've been saying the same thing every day for the last four days."

"I figure if I'm wrong enough, one of these times, I've got to get it right." Levi chuckled. "I didn't say it was gonna be easy, and you wanted to come, remember?"

"I don't regret coming," Forrester said. "I knew it was going to be challenging. That's exactly why I came, and I'm still up to it. I was hacking on you for being wrong so many times. You're the one trying to outdo all the other mountain men, aren't you? Not me—I'm just along for the ride and following orders." Now it was Will's turn to laugh.

"You just watch," Levi said. "It's been two weeks, so I figure we're just about where we wanna be, somewhere between the big Crow and Ute camps. I doubt anybody's been up here—at least not this winter. I haven't seen a sign of humans for ten days. I can't imagine anybody being this far off the grid and trappin' this far into winter. Maybe some trappers lower down the mountain, but I can't see anybody but us up here."

"Rusty also said clever Indians don't leave any signs." Forrester smiled as his blue eyes twinkled. "I've heard you say you can travel without leaving a trail. I guess if you can, most Indian warriors can too."

"And where do you get off sayin' I've been wrong every time till now?" Levi asked. "There were creeks in the other places we stopped. There just weren't any beavers. I can't help if they're findin' places farther away from man every year. I'd run too if folks were hidin' steel jaws on my path home."

They reached the summit between two tall peaks and raced down the other side. Levi made a dash for the tree line at the valley's edge. Dot trotted behind him as he jogged, but Bessy was tired, and no matter what Forrester did, he couldn't get her past a walk. She was more stubborn than most. The mules needed a rest just like Will did, but it seemed that the deeper they got into the wilderness, the stronger Levi Johnson got. It was like his body fed off Mother Nature, the challenge he had chosen.

This time, when they walked through the thick stand of trees, they found the stream they were after. It was wide enough to allow for dams without blocking it off, and deep enough that it wasn't completely frozen over yet. Small ponds branched off it everywhere beaver had made a home. Still, they could see the water flow underneath the cover of ice in the shallows, and it was thick enough to walk on, even though the surface was slowly softening due to the unusually warm fall. They could see the earth where the snow had melted in some places.

"What'd I tell ya, pilgrim?" Levi grinned. "Just like I said, here it is. Let's follow it into the valley and see if we spot any beaver dams. I betcha a gold coin there's beaver down there."

As they trekked from one end of the valley to the other, they found numerous dams creating small ponds where the water backed up. The streams were frozen solid, but they also found the entrances on the creek banks where the beaver came and went to and from their homes.

"It's gonna be hard work breakin' up those dams with the ice so thick," Levi said. "It's a good thing we've had that warmer spell of weather to make the ice softer. We've got to set the traps on the paths where they come and go, then break up the dams to force the beaver out. I figure we've got enough pelts here to load down both mules. In four or five weeks, we should be headin' back to the compound with plenty of furs to sell at next summer's Rendezvous."

Levi looked all around them but didn't see any movement. At least to the next tree line; beyond that was too far for the naked eye. Forrester pulled out his army spyglass and searched all around them for signs of danger, but he, too, came up with nothing. Still, they took their time and scoured their surroundings for signs of movement or flashes off glass or metal, even silhouettes on the horizon.

"It looks like we're alone this time," Levi said. "It still rubs me wrong that the Crow took over my find. There was plenty of beaver there too. If it weren't for that, we wouldn't have had to come all the way up here to find plentiful beaver."

"Yeah, but it was on their mountain," Forrester said. "Hopefully, this valley doesn't belong to anybody. You'd have invented some reason to go off in the middle of winter anyway."

They found a place out of the wind and unloaded and fed the mules. They hobbled them and let them dig at the snow with their hooves, trying to find some dried grass. They used an axe to chop a hole in the ice to get fresh water. Both mules drank their fill straight from the creek. The current still flowed underneath.

"If we cut down those long thin pines and clear the branches, we can make us a lean-to to have some shelter if the weather changes," Forrester said. "If we make it up against that rock, we can build a fire so we're warm enough to clean the pelts by the light of the fire at night. The fire should heat the rock, and the rock holds the heat for a while at least."

"We're gonna be busier than a three-legged mule at a butt-kickin' contest." Levi laughed.

Will stared at his friend, amazed. He didn't seem at all tired and was laughing in the face of a mountain of work. He had seen him just as brave in the face of death, from both evil White men and warrior braves. He never seemed to lose his confidence or direction. Forrester wondered if he would ever achieve such a domination of the wilderness. He sure as heck hoped so.

"You have more energy than the sun has rays of light," Forrester said and laughed too.

Now they had found what they were looking for. That was the most challenging part of the journey. At this point, it was just a matter of some hard work and a few cold nights. Then they would head back to the warm cabin to spend the deep winter in the warmth of four walls and a fireplace. There, they even had the luxury of an outhouse. With the little they had back at the compound, it now seemed like a lot. Roughing it in the winter wasn't an easy task. Especially if the weather suddenly turned.

In just a few days of hard work, from dawn to dusk, they had built a solid shelter for themselves and another for the mules. If the weather went south, they were ready. They had a string of twenty traps out and were collecting beaver every day. They had hit the bonanza Levi was searching for. As the days passed, the pile of beaver pelts got so big it didn't fit in the shelter, so they started to store more in the provisional stables.

Eventually, they had to stack them outside. Everything was frozen stiff anyway.

They had to skin the beaver on the spot before their bodies got stiff and rigid. Then the wet pelts froze on the way back to their shelter. They had to thaw them out by the fire to work them at night. It was a bloody and smelly business. Forrester suffered his way through, but for Levi, it was the bread and butter of every day back in Indiana. He hunted most of the family's food during his youth. That included the cold winter months too. That was his favorite—raccoon season.

He remembered the family dogs, Blue and Toby. Now, his father would have taken over the job again. He wondered how his mother was. Even though he was living his dream, he still missed his family. They weren't obsessed and wicked like Forrester or orphans like Rusty Steel. Levi had come from a healthy, happy home where the family relied on each other. He planned to return to see his folks one day before it was too late. He promised himself.

"It's hard to believe that we haven't run into a single problem," Forrester said as he raked his long blond hair back with his fingers. "We haven't caught sight of another human being since we left. Except for the dead Indians back at the burial grounds."

"You would have to bring that up again when I was just beginnin' to feel good," Levi spat. "I'm gonna be nervous for the next three hours."

"It'll be time to head back down in a week," Will said. "The mules won't be able to carry the load if we don't stop trapping. I believe we will have our quota in six or seven days, don't you?"

"I hate to go when the gettin's so good," Levi said,

"but you're right. We can't trap what we can't get to the compound. We don't wanna trap this spot out too much anyway. Now, we have a place to come back to that nobody knows about."

"Don't count your chickens before they're hatched." Will smiled. "But we have plenty of pelts to take to the Rendezvous, brother. All we have to do is take one step at a time. This week we'll finish up, and on Monday, we'll start back down. We won't be looking for anything or be in a hurry, so I can make my maps on the way back."

For Levi, the words were like rain after a long drought. Levi Beaver Johnson cackled with enjoyment. His mind was ultimately at rest when it came to him with sudden clarity.

"I think we did it, and we're safe. For now..." Johnson said as his eyes twinkled. "I told ya we could do it. I can't wait to see the faces of Rusty and Angus. Dennis and the boys too. I doubt any of them thought we could really do it. You and me, pard—you and me."

The men were tired but still felt good about achieving their goal. They had to collect beaver for a few more days, pull all their traps, and load the mules. Two weeks later, they would be back home and successful beyond their dreams if nothing unexpected happened. But both young mountain men felt they were on a winning streak.

They both fell into the trap of a man with expectations in the wilderness. It was a dangerous thing expecting everything to work its way out. A man with expectations would always be disappointed. That was why a good mountain man didn't expect anything. He took each day as it came—one day at a time.

Levi sighed. Forrester was an affable-looking, buck-skin-clad man; despite his size, Johnson was too. But the difference was apparent at first sight. Will was at home in an element foreign to him. He had learned to live with it. Johnson, on the other hand, was, for all appearances, more at home here than he was even in the compound. The harder it got, the better he seemed to like it. Living in the wilderness came so naturally to him that Forrester wondered how it felt.

Then again, he grew up in a big city and studied at the most prestigious university in the country. And for what? Will remembered his uncle and the Crow Indians' faces when they saw him. He came from the same gene pool. He wondered what he was capable of if he was pushed too far. He hoped whatever had been in his uncle's blood wasn't in him. Not a single drop.

Forrester put on a brave face and kept up, and he was even happy with their achievements—especially with the handicap of having only one arm to fend for himself in the wilderness.

SCALPERS

FIVE MEN SPIED ON THE LEAN-TO IN THE DISTANCE. THE two mountain men trapping the streams lost in the wilderness were unaware they were being watched from afar. Paul Dungun peered through his spyglass, following the two silhouettes as they came and went from the small provisional shelter to the streams to collect the daily beaver that filled their traps. He smiled as he collapsed his telescope and stuffed it in his pouch.

They had stayed in the same cave they found on the way up the mountain to the small Indian villages they had been told about by a deceitful Crow Indian. The information cost, but it had been well worth the old rifle. Paul wouldn't be surprised if it didn't blow up in their faces. They were there having breakfast when they discovered movement in the valley below.

Paul had been scouting the mountainside for more Indians before they headed farther back down. Dungun believed that a man could never get enough money, and collecting Indian scalps was an easy way to earn. Especially when the government was paying the bill, and there was nothing the law could do to stop them.

"Why don't we go down there now right now and steal the pelts they've got while they're away?" Grover asked. "There ain't nobody to stop us. They're just sittin' out there by their lonesome. Then we can stay on schedule and get out of these mountains before we get caught by a blizzard."

"Better yet, let's wait and let them do the work for us, and when they're done, we'll steal even more pelts," Paul said. "We ain't in any hurry iffin they be doin' the work for us, nincompoop. You've got to learn to use your noggin, fool. I don't wanna wade in any freezing' rivers —do you?"

"Put more wood on that fire, boss," Grover said. "I'm getting cold sittin here watchin'. I need to move my feet, or my toes are gonna freeze."

"Yeah, well, you just do like Paul says. We'll just sit back and watch," Herman said as he picked his nose and wiped it on his britches. "I hate work anyway. The trek up here was enough to put me off. Let them fools wade in that cold water and fetch them beaver. They skinned 'em for us and all. I'm fine doin' as Paul says. I hate work." He pulled off his fur cap and pushed a few strands of hair over a bald dome. "I even find thinkin' tirin'."

"You're so lazy you'd make a turtle look like a road-runner," Paul growled. "When God was givin' out brains, you thought he said trains, and you asked for a slow one."

"Why are ya always pickin' on me, Paul?" Herman asked.

"Because iffin I don't hack on ya, you'll go and do

somethin' stupid, that's why," Paul retorted. "Y'all are as dumb as four marbles in a tin can. Iffin it weren't for me, you'd never be successful at stealin' nothin'."

"How much do you think all of them pelts be worth?" Herman's smile displayed a mouthful of yellow plaque and black spots on scaley teeth.

"A pretty penny, I dare say." Paul grinned. "All of them furs, along with the Indian scalps—we'll make twice as much as last season thievin' and killin'. I'd never even thought of robbin' the trappers. Maybe we'll make more money from the furs than the scalps. One is gonna be as easy as the other."

Moaning came from the back of the cave. The Crow woman was tied hands and feet. Every time the five men took their eyes away from her, she struggled to get free. Paul harrumphed and stood as he twisted wax into the long ends of his drooping mustache. His eyes gravitated to the handsome woman. She was tied to a rock so that she couldn't get away.

None of the men knew who she was. They believed she must be the wife of one of the braves whom they killed in their ambush. They never even knew the scalpers were there. The lack of experience made the woman war chief make a mistake. In the wilderness, all it took was one lapse of judgment. She should have smelled them, even though they were upwind.

"Shush, you noisy fool," Paul spat at the woman. "If you keep makin' all that racket, I'm gonna have to knock you out again."

Then he drew back his boot and kicked her hard in the gut. She doubled over and gasped to get her breath. She had the wind knocked out of her. Despite the pain, her eyes were full of anger, even fury. By the look in her

eyes, it was clear she would kill the White men if she
had a knife and got close enough. Still, none of them
sensed the danger. They had killed lots of Indian
women, and none of them ever fought back.

Actually, the only Indian women they had anything
to do with they had killed as soon as they saw them
trying to flee. The difference with her was that a bullet
had grazed her head, leaving her confused, dazed, and
finally unconscious.

Initially, when they found her after they had killed
everybody else in the small band of travelers, they didn't
even know what kind of Indian she was. Yet, she had no
doubt what these men were and what they planned to
do. Up till now, though, they had struggled to keep her
tied up.

She was as wild as a mountain lion and was probably as dangerous if armed, so they kept their weapons
out of her reach even with her tied. When Paul saw how
wild she was, he wondered if he should just shoot and
scalp her and get it over with. But his lust was more
than his common sense could deal with.

She was so stunning that Paul took the chance, and
they took her with them. Even if they ended up killing
her, she would be worth a scalp. Maybe if she was lucky,
he would take her for his woman; if she struggled too
much with him, he would give her to his men to do
what they wished. Maybe that would take out that
spunky attitude of hers.

All five men wore scalps on their belts, and some
wore ear necklaces. They didn't even try to look like
anything but what they were. They were scruffy despite
their heavy fur coats. Flintlock pistols protruded from
their belts, and they carried knives in their boots. Five

mules stood hobbled not fifty feet from the group of scalpers. Several large bundles of hair lay at the entrance to the cave.

A big fire crackled and popped as they huddled around the warm orange coals. They could watch the mountain men from where they sat. Paul pulled the spyglass out again, pushed his straight black hair out of his face, and had another look. Steel-gray eyes stared into the distance. Then he passed the telescope to Grover.

They were in the shade of the cave, so there was no risk of a reflection from the glass. The mouth of the cavern was on the side of a tree-covered mountain, and snow covered that. A hint of smoke was barely visible and only on close inspection with a spyglass. The wind covered any hints of sound the scalpers might make.

There were five heavily armed men. They attacked small tribes of forty to fifty Indians, including the elderly, women, and children. The government paid less bounty for the children's scalps, but as far as the scalpers were concerned, it was still easy cash.

"Sometimes, Indians are just jealous of how simple a White man's brain is," Paul said as he stared at Henry, who was as dumb as wood. "Your problem is your brain's been picked like a chicken bone. There ain't nothin' in there but mush."

"You have no right to talk to me like that," Henry retorted. His teeth looked like they were from an exhumed corpse.

They watched the two mountain men toil for a week after they stumbled upon them. The scalpers were heading back over the mountain and down to safety before the snow hit hard. They had raided one Ute and two Blackfoot Indian camps and a small Crow war party. They killed all their members. They caught them by surprise and shot them down with their guns. In each case, it was over in a couple of minutes. It took longer to scalp the villagers than it took to kill them, much to the displeasure of Herman, who detested even the most mundane chores.

Finally, they watched as the mountain men brought the last of their pelts and returned to the streams to retrieve their traps before heading back down the mountain. The scalpers knew nothing of the mountain men or where they came from, nor were they interested in the least.

They would rather not kill them, but they would shoot them down if challenged. They were aware that most people thought scalping to be one of the lowliest trades possible. This fact made most people steer clear of them.

They weren't confused about what they did or who they had become and didn't care either. It was an easy way to make money for them, and the army paid for the scalps. It was even legal, although the Indians probably didn't take to it fondly. Paul Dungun hadn't seen much in the way of defense from the hostiles. Most of the ones he had seen were running away when they shot them in the back.

Dungun turned his eyes to his men and asked, "Anything else ya wanna talk about? I can smell the wood a-burnin'."

"Nobody's got reason to complain, boss," Herman said. "So far, it's been as easy as fallin' off a log. Those scalps are just like money. All we have to do is get them to the frontier forts in Kansas."

The Indians they had killed were nothing like they had read in the newspapers. Most publications pictured them as dangerous and cunning, something none of the scalpers had witnessed. None of the small villages they attacked expected White men to appear so high in the mountains at this time of year. Even the Crow, Ute, and Blackfeet traveled little in the deepest winter months.

"Get your tails down there right now," Paul Dungun spat. "Take your mules so you can get all the furs and try to do it before the pair of mountain men return. I'll keep an eye on 'em with the spyglass, and iffin they turn around and head your way, I'll shoot a round off to warn ya. If that happens, I'll head down and hit 'em with my rifles while you boys give it to 'em with your pistols. I figure we'll make short work of 'em iffin they do get too snoopy."

"And what they gonna think when they find their pelts stolen?" Herman asked, puzzled. "They may get angry and come after us."

"They'll think the Indians got 'em, and they'll thank the Heavens they weren't there when it happened." Paul chuckled. "I reckon they'll skedaddle out of here like turkeys to the corn. Nobody's gonna expect White men up here in the winter. That's why we caught all the Indians off guard. It was a piece of cake."

Henry said, "I don't think I'd take it kindly if a—"

"Are you still here?" Dungun, the gang leader, roared. "Get the hell down there right now and stop your blabberin'! And stop talkin' idiot talk 'cause I don't speak or understand it."

Henry Horseshoe ran out of there like a scalded chicken. The gang members grabbed their mules and raced for the crude camp the mountain men had made to shelter them while they trapped the streams. In no time, the four lackeys were down at the campsite tying all the beaver pelts on the mules' backs. When they had everything secure, they scrambled back to the cave where Paul Dungun was waiting. He unfolded his tall, lanky frame. He towered over fat little Herman.

When they arrived, the boss had already cleared their camp, poured the last of the coffee on the fire, and mounted his mule. He checked the cave for anything left behind, then they broke branches from trees to cover their tracks around the cave. It was clear that they were good at the killing part, but they were very poor frontiersmen. They were lucky they were still alive, even if they did think they had it all under control.

He grabbed the woman, threw her limp body on the back of one of the mules without a load, and tied her hands and feet around the animal's belly, so she didn't fall off. It was easy, as she had fallen unconscious again. She moaned, but nobody paid any attention.

She was just some more meat to them. Whether she lived or died would depend on how she acted. The White men had no qualms about killing one more Indian before they returned.

"Let's get out of here before those two get sight of us," Paul whispered. "Come on now, make it snappy, boys. We ain't got all day. Give me the lead to that mule with the squaw on it. I don't want her out of my sight."

In minutes, they were all leading their animals down the mountains, following their gang leader. He rode with a rifle cradled in his arms. Soon, they disappeared into the trees, leaving a trail behind them that a blind man could follow.

It looked like a long sludgy white snake across the

hidden valley. The Indian woman continued to moan in her half-conscious state. They started out at a trot with total disregard for the discomfort the Crow woman experienced.

Grover Greed was Paul Dungun's right-hand man. He was the only one the boss considered to have some common sense—not a lot but just enough. Something that none of the other three possessed. The ginger-haired scalper grinned, showing three missing teeth, a broken nose, and cauliflower ears. He was an ex-boxer from back East and the gang's muscle when things got physical.

He hailed from New York City but killed a man in a fistfight and had to flee west. He ran into Paul and his gang in Kansas. He was as tall as the boss but all shoulders and muscles. His biceps looked like legs of ham and his hands like bear paws. His eyes were too close together and looked like black chunks of polished coal. Damage to the nerves in his face made him appear to have a perennial scowl. He, too, shot lurid glances at the curvy Indian woman.

Sandy Brush took up drag for the small caravan of despicable humans. Paul Dungun rode point with his red-haired friend. Herman's heart picked up when he realized he was falling behind. He ran past and to the middle of his four partners.

He finally caught up with Paul and asked, "Do ya think those two mountain men are gonna follow us, boss?" He looked back and saw their trail in the snow.

"Why, the day a couple of youngins like them catch me will be the day the sun don't come up." Paul grinned.

"They didn't look like youngins to me," Herman

huffed. "Them mountain man types get onery really quick like."

"Of all the chicken-headed, swamp water muskrats I've ever seen, you take the cake," Dungun growled. "Why don't you open up your face and put your big feet in it? Do you see anybody around us? Can ya hear anybody?"

"No, I reckon not, boss," Herman replied. "I just got a feelin' that somebody's watchin' us, is all."

"Don't you think I'd know it if somebody was snoopin' around spying on us, fool?" Paul growled. "Now, shut up. A man can't even think when your jaw's constantly flappin'."

The four men continued to walk their mules loaded with furs and scalps. The bright sun blazed down, making them squint. Only Herman had a sense of urgency, but he dared not show it, or the boss might backhand him. It wouldn't be the first time.

The gang of scalpers and thieves didn't see the Blackfeet Indians that were watching them. And the Blackfeet didn't see the Ute Indians spying on them. Beyond them, two mountain men neared cautiously. Nobody was going to steal their pelts and get away with it.

WARRIOR WOMAN

(Several days earlier)

DAHTESTE CAREFULLY LED THE WAR PARTY THROUGH THE woods. They had heard Blackfeet Indians were attacking Crow hunters and stealing their game. It wasn't unusual for women to be war chiefs in many of the Indian tribes. Some were even famous. Women like the Cherokee Sacagawea, who helped guide Lewis and Clark, or Susan La Flesche, the healer from the Omaha tribe who became a doctor.

This young war chief wasn't famous, but she had the stuff it took to become just that. She and five warrior braves crept through the wilderness, aware of all the dangers surrounding them. Their eyes darted across the trail, looking for danger. The lush vegetation was covered in snow, making it harder to spot a hiding enemy. They squinted as they searched for movement and out-of-place colors.

Dahteste was born in Chief Hachta's camp in the Rocky Mountains above the compound. But she knew little of the White men who traded with her chief. Of course, many were in such a large camp, and only a few had sat with the mountain man, Rusty Steel, the chief's friend. Right now, she was after their lifelong enemies, the Blackfeet Indians. In their camp, she was the only woman who was a war chief, but others fought as warriors beside the men. Dahteste was considered as dangerous as any man in the tribe, except Chief Hachta, of course. He was craftier than any man she had ever known.

Her great-grandfather, grandfather, father, and all her brothers were or had been warriors, but only she had proven herself a cunning leader. Of course, all the men followed her like puppies. She was the most beautiful woman in the Crow stronghold. Even though she was gorgeous, she tried to hide her beauty as much as possible. She found the fact that men only saw what was skin deep offended her.

She wanted to be respected, not a trophy like a bear's claws or a mountain lion's teeth. She would rather stay unmarried even if she ended up like the old women who tortured the captives, full of hate with their hearts soured. She believed that at least they were noble and didn't sell themselves out because of what their peers thought. She had a mind of her own, and nobody was going to change her into a camp squaw making food, shelter, and clothing for the men of the tribe. She would rather be an old maid and spend her life alone.

She wore loose men's buckskins and knee-high moccasins to hide her very shapely body. She let her hair hang over her face to hide her high cheekbones, square jaw, and firm profile. On any other woman, her slightly large nose would be ugly, but on her, it fit perfectly. She was the kind of woman men saw and couldn't help but stare. That was precisely what she didn't want from the men in Hachta's stronghold.

Many had attempted to court or sneak peeks of her in her teepee. She lived alone by her own choice. She had shunned all who had approached with the same thing on their minds. Dahteste wasn't sure she knew what love was but figured she would recognize it if it hit her, even though she felt it unlikely at twenty years old.

All her friends she had grown up with were already married and had children. She still hadn't been struck by the craving to procreate like most women. Maybe it just wasn't meant to be. She knew everybody in the tribe of an eligible age, and she wasn't interested in any of them.

Her siblings were all boys. Her mother had died giving birth to her only girl, so she lived all her youth with only males. It was natural for her to be a tomboy because she grew up more like a boy than a girl. By the time she was thirteen, she could shoot a bow and arrow, use a lance and tomahawk, and ride better than most of the men in the tribe. Many of the young braves had challenged her in the tribal games, hoping to win her heart, but none succeeded in beating her nor in winning anything other than a sound beating.

Nor had any of them had any luck with marrying her. She was almost aloof when in front of the men of the tribe. She didn't want warriors who wanted her for her looks. She wanted a man who valued who she was, not how she looked. They had no interest in her mind and only longed for her flesh.

She was already twenty years old and getting nearly too old for marriage for an Indian woman, but she didn't seem to mind. She was more focused on honing her skills and proving to the other warriors and war chiefs of the tribe that she held her position rightfully, and if anybody doubted her, she was ready to prove them wrong.

Her rosy, red cheeks shined under her big brown eyes. Her sparkling black hair hung halfway down her back. She carried a lance as she took point. They followed the tracks but knew they were too old to be reliable. They tracked old footprints hoping they would cross some fresh tracks, and then they would have a solid direction to go in. At the moment, they could only guess.

Dahteste was well-versed in hunting both wild game and men. The clicking of bear claws on her necklace was barely audible. Of course, she had killed it herself. The bear skin coat she wore she made from the beast that tried to take her life. Two black enemy scalps were sewn into her buckskin sleeves. Dark eyebrows arched over her eyes, which were full of fire and life.

Suddenly, hackles rose on Dahteste's neck as goose bumps spouted on her forearms. She held her hand up for the warriors behind her to stop. Dahteste held her breath and listened. She knew something wasn't right. That was when she smelled the rancid sweat—she immediately knew it was White men, but she also realized it too late. They had walked right into a trap.

Flashes of fire and gray smoke came from gun barrels, following chunks of lead slamming into the braves and the trees behind them. The five Crow warriors with her were cut down in seconds. More bullets peppered the ground and the foliage around her.

Her warriors lay dead in the dirt as blood pooled beneath them.

Dahteste blinked as she stared at the sky. She couldn't figure out why she lay on her back. White clouds passed between the glowing disk and the earth as her head slowly spun around and around. Dahteste wasn't sure where she was anymore or what had happened to her. Suddenly, her head began to thunder in pain. Every beat of her heart was excruciating. Confusing visions danced in her mind. The acrid smell of blood was strong in the air.

Where am I? she thought. *What happened?*

When she tried to speak, all that came out was a croak. She moved her dry lips like a beached trout. When the White men entered her field of vision, she first saw a bald man with yellow, scaly teeth grinning at her. A cold chill ran up her spine. The bullet had just grazed her head, but she survived, unlike the rest of her men, who had died instantly. They never knew what had happened. She still hadn't figured it out either. White puffs of cotton floated across her vision. She wondered why they looked so strange.

Dahteste was the sole survivor of the ambush—she had led her braves astray and would have to live with that—or maybe not. Soon, she could be just as dead as them. Her head pounded, and rivulets of claret ran down the side of her face and into the sludge-covered trail. The white snow turned red.

She blinked, trying to clear the fog that clouded her mind. She couldn't seem to see straight. She heard the men talking. They were speaking in English. She recognized it because her chief spoke the White man's tongue, and she had heard its strange sounds before.

She looked up again and saw a tall, lanky man looking into her eyes as she felt them try to crawl back into her head.

Her head spun and spun until all she saw was darkness. Her mind's eye saw what had happened in slow motion. Every detail was clear for her to see, and it repeated itself over and over again. She remembered when she was given her name, Dahteste. It meant Warrior Woman, and she wore it proudly. But was all that already past? She looked down and saw her body. It was like an out-of-body experience she didn't understand. Then the whole world turned dark red with fresh blood. That was when she lost total consciousness.

———

WHEN DAHTESTE CAME TO, she was confused. She was on the back of a mule. Her ribs hurt with each bounce. Her heart throbbed between her ears, and her mouth was so dry that her tongue stuck to the roof of her mouth. She felt like it was full of sand. Then she realized it was a gag to keep her quiet as she breathed heavily through her nose.

Mucus and sweat dripped from the tip. The war chief blinked her eyes. Her eyelids were hard and crusty, but she forced them open. Everything was upside down. The blood ran to her head and her feet, making them throb. Her hands and feet were tied too tight, cutting off circulation. She wondered if she could stand once they cut her down.

Suddenly, one of the White men spoke, and the mules stopped. She looked up and into the coal-black eyes of the man with the scaly teeth. She shuddered when he looked at her with lustful and greedy eyes. As her mind slowly began to clear, the scalper cut the rope that tied her to the horse, and she fell to the ground with a thud. Again, she saw stars. She tried to push herself up but got dizzy again, and her eyes crawled back into her head.

When she awoke for the second time, her mind cleared, and the realization of what had happened to her fell on her like an anvil—it felt as though it sat on her chest, making it hard to breathe. Scalpers had captured her, and she would probably be sold as a slave if they didn't rape and kill her first. Her eyes bugged out of her head, and she tried to scream behind the muffled gag. She could hear the five men laughing. That made her angry, and she realized they were using her suffering for entertainment, and she didn't intend to supply them with more.

She bit her lip so hard it filled her mouth with blood, and she began to snarl like a dog. It stopped her crying then and there. She even snapped her teeth the next time the man with greenish teeth neared. His face was red, and he was breathing hard. His eyes caressed her body like a hungry animal. He even sniffed her like a rat, his nose wriggling up and his front teeth showing. Another shiver ran up her spine, but she hid her fear. Instead, she showed belligerence in her eyes.

"Don't go and get the wrong idea, Herman," Paul threatened. "She's mine. I done claimed her, fool."

"I just wanna have me a little taste," Herman said as he moved his hand for the rope that held up his britches.

Herman didn't see the gun barrel when it hit him in the back of the head. To Dahteste's dismay, he fell right across her body. The smell nearly made her vomit. The gang leader used his boot to push the unconscious body off the woman.

Then he grinned at her with greedy eyes. He had saved her only to take her for himself. A pistol hung from Paul's right hand. He grinned at the Crow woman. He was almost as revolting as the one unconscious. She wondered if all White men smelled so badly. They smelled of sweat and something murky—the smell of blood.

She blinked her eyes open, and the first thing she saw were the bundles of black hair. They were the scalps from her war party. As soon as she realized this, the blood drained from her face, and she got sick, but the gag made her choke it back or drown in her vomit. Tears streamed from her eyes, but they weren't tears of sadness or pain but anger.

Her blood boiled, but she knew she had to regain control of herself, or there would be no chance of escape. If she made it to the slavers, she would probably disappear off the face of the earth like many sold into slavery.

She felt the blood rush to her face as the fury bubbled just under the surface. Every nerve in his body went dead as she thought of the warriors lost. She sucked in a bolstering breath of air. The strangest thought wormed into her brain.

Maybe the only honorable way out was to sacrifice her life while killing the leader of the White scalpers. Maybe the man with the rotting teeth too. She couldn't go back to Hachta's tribe knowing she had failed. Now, she had nowhere to go and nothing to lose.

THE UNEXPECTED

THE BLACKFEET WARRIORS HAD BURROWED THEMSELVES into the snow, and even though they were close to the five men, they appeared not to see them—at least not yet. The Indians had seen signs of the five White men's intrusion everywhere they went. They apparently made no effort to hide at all. They didn't miss the fact that all the men wore black hair on their belts, and many more hung from their mules and were stacked beside the hides. Dozens of beaver pelts were tied into bundles. A Crow squaw was bound hands and feet at the side of the camp, but they weren't interested in the woman.

The Indian braves had assembled a war party as soon as they heard the news of the massacres. Smoke signals rose from three different Indian camps—they were answered by five more. They knew they were dealing with scalp hunters. All their families had had their hair removed. Some lost wives and sons, and others daughters or friends, but everybody there had lost family or a loved one, if not more. They were all there for restitution.

For some, it would have been enough that they had trespassed on the holy burial ground. No Indian of the three tribes controlling this part of the mountains would desecrate such a spiritual place. The three groups of Indians used the burial ground to rest their wise elders, medicine men, and chiefs. This had been the way for hundreds of years.

They had several bones to pick with the killers of their tribes. They didn't intend to allow any of them to leave, dead or alive. They would stay there, buried in the mountains with their Blackfeet families. Only after days of torture would each man there have a hand in his death.

As they watched, smoke from their fire trailed into the sky. The smell of burning wood floated in the air. The wind dropped, making it easy to locate the people responsible for the murders and mutilation. They made a long deep trail like a human slug and reeked wrath on the people they encountered for money from an angry army.

At this point, the Indian Wars had been raging for years. With the muzzle-loading rifles and pistols, many of the soldiers were no match for warrior braves who were expert archers. They found most tribes challenging to subdue, especially some like the Comanche. Most warriors could shoot three arrows in two seconds.

Most encounters with hostile Indians resulted in little gain and always several casualties in the ranks of the soldiers, whether they be wounded or dead. The tribes practiced guerrilla warfare with hit-and-run tactics, making their initial losses low. Now, the army was hiring butchers to do their job when they found they couldn't.

The various tribes continued to raid across the territories. Hopefully, the war hadn't come knocking on the mountain men's door too. Usually, when one group of White men offended one of the tribes, all White men within riding distance suffered the consequences.

The Blackfoot chief turned his painted face to his small group of warriors. They were all painted for war. He nodded, and they began pushing through the deep snow on their bellies. The scalpers didn't see their approach. They were headed for a snowdrift on the other side. Hopefully, they could push through the snow and take a bead on their enemy without raising suspicion.

They burrowed through the snow on the creek's bank until they made little holes to spy on the White scalpers. Gray gun barrels stuck through the white powder protruding out the other side, but still, the White men didn't see the danger. The chief cawed like a crow when all the men were in place. Ten seconds later, all hell broke loose.

———

THE WAR PARTY of Ute warriors carefully crept up on the Blackfoot Indians. The braves before them were so focused on their enemy that they didn't keep a close eye on their backs. Now, they had a bunch of Ute watching them as they watched the scalpers. They were the same men they were hunting. They had attacked a Ute village and wiped them out too. Smoke signals blinked into the sky as the news of these attacks rocked the mountains and everyone living there.

Every Indian within fifty miles was already alerted

in a matter of minutes. The Indian tribes had the fastest communication system available in all the West. Smoke signals were quick to make with a little green wood and a wet blanket. The warriors watched as the Blackfeet moved into position to make their attack. They had arrived just in time.

The war chief looked back at his men with raised brows then pointed to the White men and the Blackfeet. Things were getting more complicated with each passing minute. His men returned his gaze with puzzled faces.

The Ute held their ground and snuck a careful peek all around them. They suddenly froze when they saw the slightest trace of movement from the opposite side of the stream but a hundred feet to their right, just above the point where the scalpers made their camp.

The Ute war chief wondered how many people were after the same men they were. It appeared they had angered more people than the smoke signals indicated. The victims' families would retaliate, but how many tribes had the scalpers hit?

The only ones left were the Crow. It wasn't healthy for Crow, Ute, and Blackfeet to meet in the same place because they were all enemies. But they had no greater enemy than the White men before them. They were their common enemy. The war chief wondered what to do next.

"Do we attack the Blackfeet first and try to eliminate the enemy now that they have their backs to us?" the Ute war chief whispered. "Or do we ignore the Indian enemy and focus on the White man? Then what will happen when the scalpers are dead? We may not have the same advantage."

"Maybe we should wait and see what happens," a tall warrior huffed. "We can always sneak back the way we came. We are like field mice burrowing through the snow. No one will see us if we don't want them to."

"Then we will have to leave the White men for the Blackfeet, and our Ute people won't get the revenge they deserve."

"But they will still be dead," the tall brave replied. "It is a wise warrior who allows other tribes to kill his enemies and not risk the lives of his own. We must see the big plan the spirits have in store for us."

"But where is the honor in that?" the Ute war chief asked.

Suddenly muzzle flashes and gun smoke covered the edge of the far bank as the Blackfeet warriors made their attack with black powder rifles and a few lances and arrows. Unfortunately, they weren't accustomed to using long guns, and their shots went wild. They aimed their weapons like they were pointing sticks and took ten minutes to reload.

The Ute Indians watched as the instant slaughter the Blackfeet had planned didn't materialize. Instead, the White men poured on the lead from so many guns that they lost count. They must have had four or five guns each. Bullets hit the creekbank like raindrops in a thunderstorm. The crack of gunfire sounded like popcorn in a skillet.

The Ute war chief signaled for his men to move back to safety and took cover. Then they, too, began slinging arrows and lances and firing rifles. They were flanking the scalpers.

Two buckskin-clad White men suddenly popped up out of the snow and ran holus-bolus for the scalper's campsite. Now, they had them all pinned down. They didn't even regard the Crow woman they had seen in the camp. If she died in the onslaught, all the better. That saved them the time of killing her later. She wasn't going anywhere anyway, all tied up.

———

"I CAN'T BELIEVE how good these four weeks of trapping have been," Forrester said. "I believed you when you said we found a bonanza, but I never imagined so many beavers lived in one valley. This was more like a miracle —one we needed desperately."

"I didn't even get a good count on the pelts." Levi laughed. It felt good to have so much success on their own in the winter. Lucky for them, real winter weather hadn't arrived yet. "We caught 'em all so quick, and for so many days, it's like a blur to me. I'll be dreamin' about beaver for the next two weeks. I wonder what the next word is after a bonanza. I ain't even sure what a bonanza means other than a big pile of furs."

"A bonanza is a godsend, a windfall, or a jackpot." Forrester smiled. "It all means the same thing. It doesn't get any better." He grinned like a mule, showing his straight, white teeth.

Will had tired of his beard and shaved it off even though it was cold. Despite it making him look less like a mountain man and more like a soldier again, he felt cleaner. But right before this trip, he had also decided he wanted to prove himself, not to Rusty, Angus, Dennis, and the men—not even to his friend Levi Johnson, but for him alone. He didn't want to look like anybody but himself, even with the missing arm. He had decided he would make it or break it, and they had gotten lucky. Now, both men would be respected for who they were.

They piled the last of the furs on the bundles as Levi said, "Let's take the mules and collect the traps so we can bundle the rest of the pelts and load them on the animals' backs. It looks like we're ready to head home." He stood back and looked at the mountain of beaver skins. "I hope they ain't too heavy for Bessy. If she comes back lame, Rusty is gonna have my hide."

"I'll believe we did it when we're back home safe in the cabin," Forrester said. "We still have two weeks of travel to return."

"If the weather goes, it'll take longer, but we've done a good job just the same," Levi said. "I'm not worried about bad weather until January or February. Then it stops all travel in the mountains. It gets too cold, and the snows too deep."

"We could still run into Indians," Will warned. He took a moment to look around. Paranoia suddenly popped into his mind. He remembered where he was.

"We ain't seen a soul for nearly a month and a half." Levi laughed. "I was worried about trespassing on somebody's country, but it appears nobody's claimed this bit of land."

They rode the mules out of their camp, but when they returned with their traps, they would have to walk the animals, so the luxury of riding would only be one way. They turned to the sun as it warmed their faces. The mules lazily made their way to the very end of the valley. The trail was sloshy with melted snow.

"At least the mules are well rested, so they shouldn't give us trouble down the road as long as we don't push them," Will said as they rode. The gentle sound of horses' hooves nearly put them to sleep. "They haven't done any hard work for a month. I can't say the same for us. My fingers are raw from working cold furs. It'll be nice sitting in front of the fire when we get home. I can barely stop from nodding off."

"Even though we've been busier than a squirrel in a nut factory, I'm kinda sorry it's already over." Levi laughed. "What more can you ask for? Fine weather, full traps, and we've even found plenty of game out this way to eat like kings all month. And not even one sighting of an Indian, so we ain't steppin' on anybody's feet."

"I do believe elk meat is my favorite." Will grinned and licked his lips. "We might want to make some biscuits for the ride. I'm already feeling hungry. With so much work, I believe I eat twice as much as normal. Working this hard like we've done for the last month, you wouldn't notice it, though."

"It's not worth the time," Levi said. "Especially with the breakfast we ate. We've already lost half the day, but I still wanna get some distance between us and here, so we'll have to do without the biscuits."

"Are you worried or something?" Forrester asked as Mister Paranoia slipped into his mind for another visit. He looked around them to ensure nobody was watching. Still, he'd had a wary feeling for the last couple of days.

"No, I ain't worried, so don't you go worryin' either." Levi laughed. "I just wanna get home and show Rusty Steel all the beaver pelts we've got; that, and the new place to trap. We can come back when the bad weather's past. Just before next spring."

"Rather than getting colder, it's been getting warmer

for the last two weeks," Will said. "I doubt we'll be so lucky all the way home. This isn't the weather I expected."

"You'd complain if somebody gave you a thousand dollars because they didn't give ya the right denominations," Levi retorted. "Give things a chance and enjoy the day while ya can. That's what Rusty's always sayin'. Live in the moment and enjoy every one, because a man's life is mostly turmoil and danger."

"Now look who's sounding like doomsday is near," Forrester snickered. "I know as well as you do that getting down the mountain is going to have its pitfalls. Nothing ever comes this easy, so we can expect to pay some taxes for what we earn. That's just how life is."

"No, that ain't what I was sayin' a-tall." Levi chuckled. "All I'm sayin' is to enjoy every minute of beauty and tranquility when ya can—act like it's the last moment you'll ever have. It's a tough life we choose to live. It'll be full of both good and bad, but that's the same for the folks back in civilization too. Everybody's life is full of hiccups, dead ends, and wrong-way streets. Except for rich folks like your family back in New York. I can't imagine y'all sufferin' much."

"No, we had to suffer something else just as bad, if not worse." Will smiled, and it twinkled in his eyes. "We had to suffer each other. That is a fate worse than fighting Comanche."

HAILSTORMS

"AND HOW'S IT Y'ALL ONLY BE TWO MEN UP HERE ALL ON your own?" Paul Dungun asked, a hint of suspicion creeping into his voice. He appeared to be the leader.

"Why, I just told you," Forrester said as cold as ice. "We ran into Comanche—twice. We're all that's left. The rest are all dead."

The statement sobered all five scalpers instantly. They all looked across the shallow water to where the Indians waited for them to stick their heads up so they could take another shot. Luckily, all they could think about was the hostile Indians attacking them.

The occasional blast was fired from across the creek. Every time one of the White men stuck his head up, an Indian took a crack at hitting him. Arrows began to come sailing in from their side but still across the stream. The creek from bank to bank was no-man's-land.

"Watch out!" Levi shouted. "There're arrows comin' from our left flank. We've got to get out of here, or we're sittin' ducks."

"If we run, half of us will die," the ex-captain said. "If we stand and fight, we have a better chance. We need more cover. We'll have to shoot the mules, and we can make breastworks."

"And who made you two leaders?" Paul growled. "We were doin' fine before y'all showed up. Nobody invited you into our camp, and nobody's gonna shoot our mules. I don't like walkin', and then there're our furs to carry. That's something that ain't gonna happen."

Paul dove for the dirt when several shots zinged around his head. The bullets came so close he could hear them crack when they whizzed by. The Indians were slowly getting used to the rifles and were beginning to home in on their targets. His eyes stretched as he looked from the Blackfoot position to the Ute and back to where they lay.

"If we don't join in and fight together, we're going to die together, and none of us are going to make it out of here alive!" Forrester roared. Even Levi was caught off guard and taken aback. "I fight Indians for a living, mister. My name's Captain William Forrester, US Cavalry, and nobody tells me what to do." He locked eyes with Paul until he couldn't hold the stare and looked away. There was something dangerous in the captain's eyes.

Something had changed in the one-armed captain with the long blond hair. His eyes were hard but as calm as a millpond. He had no question about what he had to do next. He looked at his friend, and their eyes locked for a second. They both saw the same thing. They were running out of time.

Levi peeked out of the corner of his eye to spy on the Indian woman tied at the edge of the camp. Nobody paid any attention to her with all that was happening around them, but Johnson knew she was Crow by her clothing and beads, and he felt he had to save her because of their friendship with Chief Hachta. If they could get out of this jam, he would take her back home, and maybe the chief wouldn't be mad at the mountain men any longer.

He glanced at the pile of beaver pelts and wondered when Paul was going to put them together with the hides. It was just a matter of time. Until now, there hadn't been much chance for them to think with the hostile Indians attacking, but he knew they had to do something before the scalpers realized who they were and they turned on them despite the Ute and Blackfeet.

Johnson spotted the end of a spyglass poking out of the gang leader's pocket. That must have been how they spotted him and Will; the mountain men hadn't seen them. Levi had seen the last smoke signals and knew more or less how to read them. They probably couldn't have made out their faces with the telescope, but they had to have seen how they were dressed, even though most mountain men dressed similarly to the Indians with whom they shared the wilderness.

Rusty had taught Levi a little of what he knew about smoke signals, so he knew enough to read the words trouble and death. He could piece everything else together quickly enough with the bundle of scalps on the ground and hanging from belts. They were all black but different sizes. He imagined the small ones were from children.

He knew Rusty Steel had assured them their mistake with Major Warren Forrester would pass with time. But what if it didn't? And he and Forrester were responsible for taking the major to the big camp. Maybe they wouldn't allow them to live on the mountain anymore. The first step had been to take their newly discovered streams full of beaver. That had been enough, but now he had a chance to stay in the good graces of the Crow Indians for a few more winters, at least.

Levi wondered why he felt so confident when the odds were clearly not in their favor. He didn't even have that uneasy feeling he got when danger lurked nearby. Maybe it was the confident attitude of Captain Forrester. He appeared to have become an army captain again, even if for a short time. Or would it be something that stuck?

He chanced a glance at the Crow woman, but her dust-caked black hair hung over her face. Her body was medium size but fibered, at least from what he could see in the loose buckskins. He wondered how the scalpers had captured her. Levi inconspicuously eyeballed each of the men. He assumed that the leader was the man who said his name was Paul, and the ginger would be the most dangerous. He looked for a chance to make a move.

He had no intention of waiting on the Indians, no matter what Will said. Johnson wasn't in the army, so he would do what he felt was best for them and Rusty Steel and the other men back at the compound. At the same time, he could return a favor to Hachta. Maybe one day, Levi would be his friend too. Now, he only had to figure out how to disarm the scalpers and stop the Ute and Blackfoot attacks.

All the scalpers wore scruffy clothing and smelled of sweat and blood. Their faces, hair, and beards hadn't been washed for months. Vultures circled in the sky above them. The smell of death brought the buzzards. Perhaps one or more of the Indians had succumbed to the White men's gunfire. That, or they were drawn to the raw pieces of hair so fresh they still had beads of blood on the skin where they were cut from the victims' heads.

Paul yelled for them to fire, and his four men all took shots, but they were aiming at nothing. The Indians had chosen a spot for their ambush and had superior cover. The White men had never considered the possibility of an ambush and had never sought good cover for their campsite. Levi and Will held their fire until they had something to shoot at. That was when the ginger stopped what he was doing and turned his suspicious eyes on the two strangers.

"Ain't you two the ones that were trappin' beaver in the valley?" Grover Greed asked suspiciously. He ignored the bullets whizzing by his head. A dark look spread across his eyes as the blood drained from Levi's face.

It was apparent when the light went on in his head, and he figured out the obvious. It was easy enough to see it in his eyes. He was the only one of the scalpers that was utterly calm, and the attack hadn't ruffled his feathers so much that he couldn't work out the obvious. The other four men remained oblivious to the discovery as they frantically fought the hostiles.

Grover turned and made a move for Levi. He had a pistol in each mitt. The perennial sneer on his lips got more profound. His eyes narrowed on his target. Johnson saw it in the snarl on his lips. He raised his gun as he drew back the hammer. The other four scalpers were shooting their guns as fast as they could, so they didn't see Grover go for the big mountain man.

Suddenly, Forrester had his gun in his hand, and the barrel was an inch from Greed's head. He pulled the trigger, and the gun recoiled as his brain and jaw blew out and spattered into the dirt. A half dozen teeth looked up at them from the ground. He was dead instantly and fell over with a thud. Will casually shoved the spent pistol into his belt and pulled another loaded gun. He calmly walked up behind Paul's head and pressed the barrel to the back of his neck. He started to yelp, but the captain pulled back the hammer. The click stopped him from screaming. He wet himself. Paul waited for the bullet.

Chunks of lead tore at Will's coat, but he ignored the onslaught of bullets. His attention was focused on the scalpers. All their attention turned from the hostile Indians to the strangers that had run into their camp.

Will glanced at Levi, and a single look was enough. They knew each other so well that they knew what the other was thinking. Johnson ran for the edge of the camp and instantly disappeared into the shadows. It happened so quickly that Will blinked his eyes like he couldn't believe what he saw. He had clearly turned into what the Indians called a shadow walker, just like Rusty Steel.

When the weather began to change, everybody was taken by surprise. All four parties were so focused on their mutual enemies they hadn't noticed the dark clouds behind the peaks above them.

One moment the sky was crystal clear, and the subsequent dark clouds passed the summit, blanketing the valley in deep shadows. Bolts of silent lightning shot from cloud to cloud. The air was charged with electricity. They began to hear rumbling thunder in the distance. Still, no rain fell, nor did it snow.

Suddenly, bolts of lightning began to pepper the valley before them. Trees cracked as thunder roared and ripped into the forest. The flashes of light walked toward the astounded observers. Their attention had been momentarily drawn to another more significant and violent danger.

When the thunder rolled, the earth trembled. It looked and sounded like the end of the world. A bright, beautiful day had become a nightmare under the little light that penetrated the storm clouds. Cumulonimbus soared overhead between the earth and the sun.

The first rocks of ice fell scattered across the water. They were large and made little explosions on the flat surface. As the hail grew bigger, it dented the scalper's hats and pounded the mountain men and Indians' heads and caps. Some of the chunks of ice were as big as a chicken egg. Just like that, the fight was temporarily suspended as they all ran for their lives and the shelter in the trees a short distance from the stream's bank.

Forrester pulled the heavy grizzly bear coat over his head and stayed where he was. He kept his guns under the fur coat to keep the powder dry. The pounding hail made a deafening sound, making it impossible to speak or hear.

Ice balls thudded into their thick coats and hats, but the dense fur absorbed most of the impact. Indians scattered and sought shelter beside tribes that were their enemies. Yet they were all enemies of the White men, at least with the scalpers.

"Now, what are we gonna do?" Paul asked.

"Enjoy the fact the weather saved our bacon, at least for now!" Will yelled over the pounding hail. Suddenly, he held a knife to the gang leader's neck. Herman, Sandy, and Steve stared at the captain as the hail turned into snow.

Their eyes flashed from their dead red-haired friend on the ground and back to their boss with a massive knife blade tight against his neck. Every time he moved, Will applied more pressure to the Bowie knife.

SHADOW WALKER

LEVI RAN FROM THE SCALPERS' CAMP, DISAPPEARING instantly. He moved from one shadow to another, only leaving his image to be seen for a fleeting second. He hid in the dark places between the light and the shadows, moving deeper into the brush and nearing the wide stretch of creek, and looked at the other side. He crawled closer to the water.

Beaver Johnson quickly located the position of both sets of attackers, but he had to wait until he got glimpses of each group. How many were there in all? He already knew one group had rifles and the other nearly none, but this didn't give him any idea of their danger. As he waited and watched, he quickly saw there were far too many warriors to defeat on their own. They had to escape somehow.

Johnson knew the White men in the camp were scalpers, and he knew the Indians knew it too. Everybody within fifty miles would have seen the smoke signals. Only the White men didn't know of the alarm.

All the tribes in the mountains would know every detail by now.

Soon, there would be nowhere to hide, so they had to kill the rest of the scalpers or leave them to the Blackfeet and get away with the Crow prisoner. They had to find some way to escape. How had they gone from such a beautiful day to what they had before them now? His mind raced to find a solution as he continued to crawl.

If only the scalpers hadn't stolen their pelts, they could walk away from the whole situation and leave it to the tribes to sort out. He didn't think the scalpers had a chance. But then again, there was the woman. It dawned on him right then that there was no way he could walk away, no matter what happened. All it took was one look at the ruffians that abducted her to know what would happen if they did succeed in winning the day. That was assuming some wickedness hadn't already happened.

Levi felt like he had to run off and save any women in distress. He fondly remembered his mother. His father had taught him to respect women and never to treat them with physical violence. To Johnson, it didn't matter if she was red, white, or black. Not to mention a Crow, like Rusty's friend, Chief Hachta. No man had any right to treat a woman like an object. He knew what the scalpers had in store for her before they sold her like the bloody mats of hair they stored in bundles. How many Indians died to make such a mountain of scalps?

Suddenly, the sky erupted into chaos. Thick, dark clouds covered the heavens, blocking out the sun. Lightning peppered the earth as thunder rumbled. Hail fell like bullets from the sky. Across the stream's surface, balls of ice exploded like small bombs.

Johnson's heavy bearskin coat and raccoon cap protected him from the ice projectiles. He used the moment of confusion to cross the stream. He held his pistols high as he kept his head and guns just over the surface of the deep water as he raced for the other bank.

As soon as he neared the trees, he again slipped into the shadows as the snow began falling. The rifle fire returned and rose into a cacophony of noise. Then it briefly stopped again. Levi snuck up behind what he saw were Ute warriors—there were only a half dozen of them. They had their arrows trained on the scalpers' camp. That's when he saw Forrester stand with his gun to Paul Dungun's head. It was such a surprise to both Indian war parties; all but a few stopped firing for just a moment. Then they resumed but with less deter-mination.

When the hail suddenly stopped, it was replaced with giant snowflakes. They fell nearly horizontal as gusts of wind carried them through the air.

Levi jumped to his feet and screamed a Comanche war cry as he shot his pistols into the sky. He bolted for the Ute warriors, who were so surprised when the giant man roared toward them that two of them jumped into the water. Those too shocked to move, Johnson swung his rifle by the barrel in a wide circle, thumping several Indians in the head.

The Ute war party was thrown into bedlam, but the other Indians weren't fazed. That was when Levi saw how many Blackfeet there were. They were more aggressive and violent than both the Ute and the Crow together and made peace with nobody. Now, he had to get back to the camp to warn Will and somehow grab the woman before the scalpers or the Indians killed her. She was their enemy too.

The cross back to the other side of the stream was more dangerous now. The Blackfeet had seen the wild mountain man scare the Ute warriors away. They probably were looking for a way out anyway. If they defeated the White man, afterward they would have to deal with the Blackfeet anyway because they, too, were their mortal enemies. But they were hopelessly outnumbered, so they had no choice but to flee.

Bullets whizzed dangerously close to Levi's head. He bit the bullet, forgot about his powder, and dove underwater as his long arms and legs quickly stroked his way to the other side. He moved so quickly through the deep stream that he looked like the beaver he was named after. He burst from the surface and raced up the bank to his partner, Forrester. He dove for cover, gulping air as quickly as he could.

"Get down, fool!" Levi Johnson screamed. "You're gonna get yourself killed acting all brash and reckless!"

When William ignored him, Levi jumped to his feet and tackled him and Paul, the gang leader, bringing them both to the ground as bullets slammed into the snow, ice, and vegetation around them.

"I don't know about you, but I wanna live until tomorrow, and I need your help to do just that," Levi huffed. "There's more Blackfeet over there than I can count, so we'd best get goin' while we still can."

"What about the scalpers?" Will asked. "What do you want to do, kill them?"

"You already killed one," Levi replied. "Ain't that enough? Let God sort the rest of 'em out with the Blackfeet. I reckon they'll do the devil's work all right."

"What about us?" Paul Dungun asked. Now, his demeanor had changed entirely, and he was scared. His eyes stretched so wide they looked like they would pop out of his head.

Levi looked at the scalper, then at the mountain of hair, and back again. "There ain't no us. Not anymore, there ain't. I'm takin' the woman with us."

"If you are, you better hurry, partner," Forrester replied calmly as if they weren't being threatened by a couple of dozen Blackfeet warriors.

Levi pulled his large knife, and the woman's eyes spread wide when he neared her. She began to sing her death song.

"I ain't gonna hurt ya," Levi said in the little Crow Rusty had taught him. "Do you speak English?"

She looked puzzled, shook her head, and trembled before the six-foot-seven mountain man. She hadn't ever met a White man that wasn't trying to kill. To her, this one looked like he might kill her too. When Levi cut the binding on her hands and feet, she looked even more perplexed. She hadn't expected anything but rape and murder, and now she felt the man cutting her ropes had kindness in his eyes. He still hadn't noticed her beauty.

She was bruised and battered. The giant White man went to pick her up. Before she could protest, he scooped her into his arms and ran into the forest with Forrester on his heels. She wrapped her arms around Beave's neck and held on for dear life.

"What about our beaver pelts?" Will asked as they ran pell-mell through the forest.

"I reckon we best save ourselves first before we plan

to take on the entire Blackfoot Nation," Levi huffed as he continued to run.

After what seemed like an hour but was probably thirty minutes, they finally stopped and dropped to the ground. The men had been running in a full sprint, and Johnson was carrying the woman. Levi gently laid her beside him, and he gobbled air.

His heart pounded between his ears. Finally, he glanced at her face, and she could see him start. She knew she had such an effect on men. Maybe this time she liked it, unlike the others. She felt gratitude rather than scorn like she usually did.

"What's your name?" Levi asked.

"Dahteste," she replied. "And you?"

She got a strange feeling when the man called Levi talked. Dahteste almost felt shy in front of a man twice her size, but he was handsome and obviously a warrior, or he would never be so brave and gallant. Despite the fact she knew they were far from safe, she felt secure with the gentle giant. She looked into his eyes questioningly, but he just got a puzzled look on his face. Maybe he was more like many men she had met in the past. Still, she felt she had to give him a chance, even if he was White.

Dahteste knew that when she returned to her tribe, she would do so in shame. She had lost all four of her warrior braves. Hachta wouldn't look at such a defeat as honorable. She should have died with her warriors. How would she explain what happened and how she was hit with a bullet, rendering her a useless leader? Especially with four dead men.

They had ambushed them perfectly, and she had led her braves right into the trap. She had only noticed the smell when it was too late for them to prepare. They were cut down before they grabbed their weapons.

She didn't know if she had been cursed by evil spirits and sent on an impossible mission. With the scalpers in the area, the situation quickly changed. Every Indian within a hundred miles probably knew what had happened by now.

She looked into Levi's eyes and asked, "The bad men? We can't let them escape."

"Oh, I doubt they be goin' anywhere, ma'am," Levi said. "The Blackfeet will take care of 'em."

She blinked her big brown eyes and said, "There are more Blackfeet. I saw their tracks from the horse when I came to for a moment. The scalpers don't know. They are stupid. Soon they will be dead."

"How many?" Levi asked, now worried. His brow furrowed, and his eyes narrowed.

"Maybe twenty more," Dahteste replied. "More than forty in all."

"Grab your stuff, Will," Levi grumbled. "She just said there's another twenty or so Blackfeet out there. We best forget about the pelts and run for home, or we ain't ever gonna make it."

No Escape

They raced blindly through the forest. Snow-covered bushes and branches slapped their faces as they ran by, the icy powder stinging their cheeks, ears, and noses. Now, Dahteste sprinted beside Levi as his long legs blurred, but somehow, she kept up. She was as fit as the two mountain men, if not fitter.

Levi noted her feline-like body as she moved with such agility. She was as graceful as a deer and nearly as fast. Will had his mind on something else and had hardly noticed that the captive was a woman and a beauty at that. All he could think about was wreaking revenge on the scalpers and the Blackfeet Indians for stealing their hard-earned beaver pelts.

He wasn't ready to run like Levi, but for the woman's sake, he folded and went against his instincts to stand and fight, but that didn't mean he liked what they were doing. His mind churned for a plan to get the furs back, but he knew if there were more Indians looking for scalpers, they would have little chance of escaping detection.

One second, Levi was running as fast as his legs could take him, and the next, he dropped to the ground and dragged both Dahteste and Forrester with him. They tumbled in the snow. They all heard the noise now as the other war party made its way through the forest. They were right in front of them, so all three froze.

They carefully chanced a peek as they pushed their heads above their cover. Suddenly all around them, Blackfoot warriors popped up out of the snow. It had been a trap prepared in case the scalpers escaped, but the mountain men had fallen right into it. The Blackfeet Indians were buried in white powder and waiting to spring the trap.

The one-armed officer glared at the Blackfoot Indians standing around them, armed with both guns and arrows. They were all painted for war. The blood drained from Levi and Dahteste's faces. The captain's eyes flashed with violence. He didn't seem to care. He acted like he was ready to take on all twenty braves. It looked like he dared the hostiles to cut him down, but you could see in his eyes that he planned to take several with him. He grasped his saber in his left hand but didn't have a chance.

Behind the men stood Dahteste, the Crow war chief. She took a step forward. She had no way to protect herself from certain death at the hands of the Blackfeet Indians. Her eyes spread wide with fear, but there was anger and rebellion there too. She refused to cry or lose hope. She, too, wanted to take one of the warrior braves with her to the grave.

"Hold on there, old pard," Levi whispered out of the corner of his mouth as beads of sweat popped up on his brow. "We don't wanna push these boys into doin' some-thin' we'll regret, now do we? Now, you two raise your hands so they know we don't wanna fight 'im. And put that sword away, or they shoot ya before you take a step. They can't be that bad of shots at this range, so I reckon iffin they all shoot, one of 'im is gonna kill ya."

He turned to the Blackfoot woman, but one look was enough. They didn't have to speak. She knew what was happening now. Still, she pulled herself into Levi's side as he frowned at the enemy.

He pulled the woman behind him to protect her body with his. She wrapped her arms around his waist and burrowed her face into the small of his back. Johnson towered over her. Will slipped his saber back into its sheath. The leader of the war party said some-thing in Blackfoot, and warriors instantly swarmed them, and they roughly grabbed them, and dragged them back to where they'd fled.

The Blackfeet had already captured the other four White men when they reached the scalpers' campsite. One had already been scalped alive. He screamed as his hands patted his head for hair but only came away bloody, then he passed out.

It appeared that the ginger outlaw was the man who had bolstered their bravery in a fight, and without him, they were just four more terrified White men in the clutches of hostile Indians—even Paul, the gang's leader. Now, they would pay for their sins and crimes against man and the Almighty.

———

LEVI AND FORRESTER sat on the ground with their hands tied together and to their feet so they couldn't stand. Blackfeet Indians surrounded them and poked them with sticks. They didn't see the small straight razor in Johnson's boot. He struggled as he watched the warriors cut the ropes on the Crow woman. Their eyes were full of lust. It was clear what they had planned. The Crow Indians were mortal enemies of the Blackfeet so they would show her no mercy.

Levi struggled with his bindings as his blood boiled. His muscles flexed, and he ground his teeth as he struggled to escape. The Indians found his anger funny, and they poked him some more with sticks and jeered at him as they laughed. The other three White men were tied, spread eagle in the snow. Minor wounds covered their bodies and seeped blood into the snow. The red and white contrasted.

Will Forrester stared at his best friend like he was watching a folly of life utterly detached from the present. He showed no fear at all and almost smiled when the Blackfeet warriors poked at him with spears and sticks. But they could all see the hate in his eyes. If they let him free for a second, he would take a life even if he only had one hand.

Levi grabbed the blade of the razor and hid it behind his legs as he used his fingers to saw at the rawhide. It was wet from the slush and tightened with each effort. His eyes pleaded with the Blackfeet Indians to leave the woman alone, but their interest was elsewhere, and they had forgotten the mountain men for the moment.

"We've gotta do somethin', Will," Levi growled. "I'll be out of these ropes in five more minutes."

"I don't know if Dahteste has that much time," Forrester observed. His voice sounded far away. He had accepted the fact that he would soon die. All he wanted to do was take as many Blackfeet warriors with him as he could. Maybe he would have a chance to kill the woman, too, before a dozen or more braves soiled her.

Forrester looked around and frowned. They were surrounded by nearly forty painted faces, all brimming with bloodlust. Once they finished with Dahteste, he knew they would come to torture and kill them. He remembered what an old captain had told him when he arrived at the frontier forts to take over his company as captain. He had told him never to let the Indians catch him. It was best to shoot yourself before the punishment they would give you if they caught you alive.

He had already seen what they were doing to Paul, Herman, Sandy, and Steve. Lucky for Horseshoe, he didn't have a scalp to take. One thing Forrester knew for sure was that he wouldn't die like that. He would die fighting like a soldier. He tried to ignore Levi as he cut his bindings, so he didn't draw attention to his actions. He knew they were out of time.

A sudden anxiousness came over him. Destiny had finally caught up with him. When he lost half the men in the expedition, he thought he should have died with them and not survived. So, it looked like the mountains were going to take his life anyway, too. It hardly bothered him, but he also hated to witness his friend's death. He hoped he went first, or they might go together in a blaze of glory. He chuckled, and Levi looked at him quizzically.

Now, he didn't have to worry about being discovered again like his uncle, Major Warren Forrester, had done.

If he had survived, one day, he knew he would have to return to face the music. Now, all that was taken care of. All he had left was to die a brave death. He hoped that wasn't too much to ask after all was said and done.

Levi felt the blood rush to his face as his heart sped up, pattering in his chest.

Johnson surprised his friend when he asked, "Did you feel anything when you shot the scalper?"

"Sure, I did," Forrester said, smiling. "I felt the recoil."

"You're crazier than a mule humpin' a goat," Levi said as he smiled at his friend. "Standin' there with all that army officer crammed inside ya burnin' to get out. We sure do make a strange pair of partners."

"What about the Crow woman?" Will asked. Now he was serious again.

"She's goin' with us, pig or pork—even if it means dyin' with us," Levi replied, his mouth a brutal gash. "Anything will be better than what she's about to face. I'm gonna get ugly on these fools like an ugly ape and turn 'im every way but loose. I always figured we'd go out in a blaze of glory."

"Really?" Forrester grinned. "At least we became mountain men before our time was up. I wonder if anybody will remember us."

Right then, Levi managed to cut through the heavy leather holding the handle of the straight razor between one finger of each hand. The rope fell to the ground, but he didn't move. He flicked the razor to his partner when no one was looking. Will began cutting at his bindings. In minutes, they would both be free. When his rope fell off, he stood and pulled a pistol from under his coat in the small of his back.

Levi's eyes grew when he saw the large barrel of the gun.

"We must be out of our minds," he said as he stood. He towered over everybody.

Forrester aimed and fired. A flame and gun smoke followed the chunk of lead and struck the leader right between the eyes. His men were so shocked that they all stopped as they watched their war chief die on the ground before them. Blood pooled under his body from the gaping wound in his face. He was dead as soon as the bullet hit. Will held his ground as all eyes turned on him. They were all full of anger and violence.

While their attention was diverted, Levi broke into a run toward the four Blackfeet dragging Dahteste to the edge of the forest. They tried to tear her buckskins off, but she fought like a rabid cat. Johnson saw her clawing and biting every inch of the way. He was on them before they noticed. He sliced at the warriors with the straight razor he had retrieved from Forrester.

The four Indians dragging Dahteste away turned on the large man coming for them. They dropped her into the dirt, dazed, and turned to fight, but all four of them went down like German ninepins in an alley. Levi's fists were a flurry, and the small steel blade flashed in the sunlight. Blood spurted from one neck, and another clutched at his throat as his neck was cut. It happened so quickly that they were all caught off guard.

The attention had been diverted from the struggling woman. Now, they had a new focus of attention. The two crazed White men killed the braves as fast as they could reach them. The chief yelled, and all eyes turned to the mountain men. Levi stood over Dahteste as she lay where they left her. He looked like a rabid wolf standing over his woman, fending off all those who advanced.

Just as suddenly, two dozen guns pointed Levi's way. He stopped, grabbed Dahteste in his arms, and held the blade to her neck. He would take her life before he allowed them to take her from him again. Then he would wreak the wrath on them all until he, too, was dead.

He saw Forrester out of the corner of his eye. Somehow, he had gotten ahold of his sword again and quickly lopped off the heads of two Blackfeet. Indians. They rolled across the ground to the horror of their fellow braves. Everybody turned on the White men, who stood back-to-back with the Crow woman at their feet. They were ready to fight to the finish. All three were ready to die.

RUSTY & ANGUS

THEY KNEW THEY HAD TO INTERVENE AS SOON AS THEY saw the relayed smoke signals from the Crow camp. Rusty was an expert at reading Indian signs of all types, especially smoke signals. They could be rather detailed if you knew how to read them well. The first warning he and Angus saw was the word of the butchered Blackfoot and Ute Indians, families and all. Shortly after came the word that a small Crow war party was massacred to the last man. Nobody knew anything else of War Chief Dahteste or her fate.

They hadn't seen only one set of signals either; there were many during the course of three days. Most of them came from Hachta's camp. One of his war chiefs had been abducted by scalpers. The Ute warriors were reporting every action back to their stronghold. The Indians used relays to send messages long distances. The source of information would be sent up in smoke, and the relay post would read them and send the message to the next relay. Hachta always said the Ute talked too much for their own good.

With this system, in hours they could inform their people and, in this case, three tribes of all the events up to that day. Their mountain man youngsters were just about to be overwhelmed by the Blackfeet warriors. Or maybe they had already fallen to the White men who killed women and children for their hair.

"Get the mules ready, Angus," Rusty said. A sense of urgency was in his voice. "We're gonna have to get those young boys out of trouble. I'll go round up Dennis, Sam, Bob, and Pete. From the smoke signals, I have a pretty good idea of where they are. They must have traveled over hell and half an acre to get there, but as the crow flies, it ain't all that far. I'll go make a fire so I can send a message to the Crow camp. Lucky for us the Ute tend to blabber about everything they do, so there ain't no secrets on this mountain. I reckon they got the woman iffin she's still alive."

LEVI AND FORRESTER stood back-to-back—one with only a straight razor in his white-knuckled fist and the other with his officer's sword. Several Blackfeet Indians lay bleeding or dying at their feet, but now the rest of the warriors all turned their weapons on the White men and the Crow woman. Now that they saw how well they fought, they knew they had to tread carefully, or they, too, would succumb to their blades.

A dead war chief lay at the mountain men's feet, and the eyes of their enemy begged for revenge. They knew they weren't going to make it out of there alive.

Levi grabbed Dahteste close to his body and whispered in her ear in Crow. "I promise I won't let them get to ya. Don't worry, I'll make it fast. It won't hurt."

Johnson's eyes were filled with regret. Dahteste was putting on a brave face, but she was just about to lose control. She knew all their fates were sealed, and they were about to die.

She touched Levi's face, kissed his cheek, and said, "It will...be fine." She tried to smile but failed miserably. Her face was as pale as death. "We will soon be together in the spirit world. It is written in our destiny. It is written in stone."

Right then, he felt he had never been so close to a woman even though they had just met. With all that was happening, they felt they had known each other all their lives. They exchanged knowing looks, and both joy and sadness were in their eyes. He felt joy that they had somehow found each other. At the same time, he felt sad it would only last a few more seconds before they would all soar with the eagles and pass into their spirit worlds.

Levi suddenly wondered if a White man could fly in the spirit world like an Indian or would he be sent to another destiny. Hopefully, it would be heaven and not hell. Johnson wondered if Dahteste would go there too. There were too many questions and too little time to acquire the answers. Now, minutes passed like they were seconds as the time flew by. They knew they only had a few breaths of life left. Soon life's suffering and pain would be past, and they would rest in peace forever.

Beaver touched his best friend's shoulder and looked into his eyes. Behind the fury, he saw regret too. Nobody was ready to die when the time came. That was something he had just realized. He had been near death before but hadn't had time to think. Both times he'd been fighting wild animals and Comanche, but even then, he was never so close as now, and he knew there wasn't anything they could do. He heard a clock ticking in his head. It was just about to stop. Tears welled in his eyes as he put pressure on the blade against Dahteste's neck.

"Goodbye, darlin'," Levi said as Dahteste looked at him puzzled—then she smiled knowingly but kept her brave face. She was a Crow warrior, after all. This was the death she had waited for all her life. She felt both fortunate and robbed to have found her man, almost too late even to know a man was out there waiting on her.

Suddenly, Levi howled like a wounded wolf. He became consumed with anger as he turned his eyes on his enemy. In his fur coat, he looked like a giant grizzly bear himself. When he roared, it sounded like another beast in the forest, but this was the cry of a wounded animal.

He held the blade to his woman's neck. A rivulet of blood ran down her neck, and a tear cut a clean streak down her dust-covered face. But still, she stood firm and tall. She was a proud Crow warrior, and she refused to show fear in the face of her enemy. She wouldn't give them the pleasure of seeing her frightened.

Johnson's hand trembled slightly as he tightened his grip on the straight razor. He knew what he had to do, and even though it would be the hardest thing he had done in his life, he was aware it was the only way to see that Dahteste didn't suffer the rape and beating the Blackfeet Indians planned for her. He had to make sure they would both die first. Will would have to do his own bidding. Dahteste began to sing her death song. Now, it was in earnest. Forty hostile Indians stared at the three captives just before they went to rush them.

The warriors ignored the three men tied to stakes in the ground. Their clothing had been ripped from their bodies, and they lay shivering in the nearly freezing temperatures. Their hands and feet were black from lack of circulation and combined cold. The Blackfeet would have to hurry, with the three still struggling to survive. If not, the White men tied to stakes would die from exposure, and they would lose their opportunity to torture them as planned. The end was just about to play out.

————

RUSTY STEEL and Angus McFarlin pushed their mules as hard as they dared. Their lungs sounded like a blacksmith's bellows as the animals struggled to breathe. They were ready to run them into the ground if they had to. They had to make it to their young friends before their Indian enemies took their lives, if they hadn't already.

Sweat glistened on all six mountain men's faces and their mules' necks as they raced to rescue the new additions to their compound. These young men were now their brothers, so they were ready to give their lives for them. Just like Levi and Will had previously endangered their lives for the older mountain men.

Each carried four pistols in their leather belts, two rifles in scabbards on their mules, and another across their laps. They were armed to the teeth and ready for whatever happened. Large Bowie knives protruded from their boots.

Rusty had a bow strapped across his back with a quiver of arrows. Angus wore a hat made of buffalo horns. It made him look twice his size and unusually fierce. The mules raced up and down steep trails and across snow-covered valleys. The only sounds were huffing lungs and the soft steps of horses' hooves in the crunchy snow. Nobody exchanged a word. There was nothing left to say.

They all focused on the trail ahead except Yosemite Bob. The short, gray-haired old mountain man with the handlebar mustache that drooped below his chin rode drag. He ensured none of the Blackfeet Indians snuck up on them from behind and caught them unawares. He was the oldest of the eight, but he, too, was ready to end his time on earth that day if he was called to the great yonder in the sky.

Rusty and Angus rode point with Dennis, Portland Pete, and Syracuse Sam following. They did their best to keep a sharp eye out for an ambush, but they knew they would surely be too late if they were too careful. So, they rode onward more recklessly than they had ever traveled. They knew time was running out. They might arrive and find them already dead. Nobody had much hope for the life of the woman war chief, Daht-este. Still, there was a little hope for the young mountain men, but not much. Too much time had passed.

They all believed Dahteste would have been the first to die. If not, she would have been raped and ruined for life. Most women who suffered such abuse from Blackfeet and lived were never the same after. They tried not to think about the woman. Rusty had seen her a couple of times, but he doubted she'd noticed his careful stare.

Rusty had never seen an Indian woman with such beauty—especially a Crow. He had to admit that the first time he saw her, he, too, was smitten despite his age. He had to stifle a chuckle when he thought of the moment in the past. Hachata had admonished him for his foolishness. He told him she was part mountain lion and part wild cat, and her name was Dahteste, which meant Warrior Woman. That was enough for Rusty to laugh at himself and dismiss his interest. She would probably be more than a man his age could survive.

The Blackfeet ditched the usual caution. They were forty strong and carried flintlock rifles and pistols, so they felt they had no equals in the Rocky Mountains. This was why they foolishly didn't even set out guards. They were sure another such force wouldn't be found in the mountains in the winter. Only fools dared Mother Nature so. They had the scalpers that survived and had already begun their torture. One was already scalped, and all four lay freezing to death on the ice-packed ground.

Now, they were about to kill the three that resisted. They already had seen that the three would never be taken prisoners, so they would die then and there. The war chief smiled, exchanged looks with his best men, and raised his lance to give the order to attack. Levi, Will, and even Dahteste were seconds away from their mortality.

When the six mountain men bolted right through the middle of the camp, firing their pistols, they caught the Blackfeet by surprise. Three Indians dropped to the ground, all dead before they hit dirt. These were trained and experienced warriors, though. They stood their ground and prepared to return fire. Six more White men wouldn't stop them from doing what they were doing. They would just add the six to the prisoners to torture.

When Chief Hachta slowly walked his horse to the edge of a nearby hill, he rode alone on a white stallion. Will's jaw dropped as he saw it was his horse. Hachta yelled something in Blackfoot then he spat on the ground. It was clearly an insult as all forty braves stopped what they were doing and turned to the lone chief. Hate burned in their eyes, and the Crow chief smiled like he had a secret none of them knew. It was so quiet that the only sound was the crows waiting in the distance. They already smelled death in the air.

Chief Hachta whistled, and a hundred warriors on Indian ponies walked into view. They completely circled the camp. Then, the chief saw Dahteste holding onto Levi like he was a piece of driftwood floating in a sea of danger—his smile turned into a grin.

"We should kill you all," Hachta growled in the silence as he frowned an ugly gash. "You killed four of my warriors and kidnapped my war chief. I will let thirty leave with their lives, but ten must stay." He turned to the man he assumed to be the leader from his dress. "You will have to pick the men who die. That will be your burden—your disgrace. You will live to return to your camp and tell the elders what happened today. You will remember not to walk on Crow ground again."

"You are out of your territory, Chief Hachta," the Blackfoot war chief spat. "You don't own all these mountains."

"I take my territory with me wherever I go," the

Crow chief snarled. "You have the time it takes the scalpers to die to make your choice. They are close to death now. Ten of your men will stay here with these scum—murderers of women and children. My braves will finish what you have started. The rest of you will go back to tell your chief what happened today. Be fore-warned—no one will leave here next time because there will be no next time. You will all die where you tres-pass." He looked at his friend Rusty and added, "Take your people and go in peace, Rusty Steel. We have saved both my war chief and your friends. It is a good day for us. Not so much for the Blackfeet."

"And my beaver pelts?" Will Forrester asked. Every-body was surprised when he spoke. "That's what we came up here for, isn't it?"

Hachta nodded and said, "Take the pelts and your mules. The rest we will take care of." The chief looked at the bundles of scalps and frowned as anger burned in his eyes.

Dahteste dared to shoot a glance at her chief. His eyes were drawn to hers, and they locked. After several seconds, she averted hers and looked at the ground as she clutched Levi's arm, and they scurried away from the danger. Forrester loaded the pelts on the mules' backs and raced behind his friends. None of the White men wanted to stay in the scalpers' camp any longer.

Rusty herded them away from the Indians like a mother hen with her baby chicks. Angus took up drag with Sam this time to ensure no danger followed. Now, they carefully picked their way through the wilderness just like always. You never knew what waited around the corner.

BUBBLY FEELING

THE SNOW HAD STOPPED, AND THE CLOUDS HAD disappeared as quickly as they had appeared. The hail-stones had melted and fused with the snow, packing it down into one layer. Now, the ground was hard to walk on, but the weight of the horses broke through the crust. The sound echoed against rock cliffs.

His-and-her hearts beat nervously as their hands touched. Levi used his fingers to brush her hair back from her face. Her cheeks were rosy red in the cold. She rode in front of him in his saddle. He held the reins with one hand and the other wrapped tightly around the woman. Their body heat kept them warm.

"I've been looking for a friend," Dahteste said in Crow as she turned and looked up at Levi. Her brown eyes seemed as big as the sky. She blinked long lashes. Her olive skin had a healthy sheen to it, although her face blushed red.

"Well, you best stop lookin'," Levi said as he stared at his woman. He smiled, and it reached his eyes. "I reckon we can both stop lookin' now."

The violence in Johnson's stare was replaced with something new for him. It was so foreign that he didn't know how to act, but he knew it was good. He felt a flush fill his face, and as he breathed, it hitched. He was even a little dizzy, like he couldn't get enough air. Dahteste smiled, and her eyes, too, twinkled with happiness.

She'd never looked at another man like she did Levi Johnson. Then again, she had never met a man like him before, and this time, she didn't intend to leave his side. He wasn't like any men who had tried to win her over before. He was one of a kind.

Now that everybody knew how the scalpers ambushed them, she knew she could return to Hachta's Crow stronghold if she wanted. For now, she wasn't in any hurry. Maybe they would go back and visit sometime during the winter—or maybe even in the spring. She would like to show him her teepee and her trophies —maybe to meet her mother and father, but she wasn't in a hurry. They had both discovered something new in their lives—each other.

Dahteste had heard about the mountain men living in the cabins in their compound. She had never seen them, though. She had caught glimpses of Rusty Steel before when he visited Chief Hachta. She knew he was said to be an honorable man. She already knew what kind of man Levi was.

He was the one who insisted on saving her, even if it meant losing his life. He was even brave enough to be prepared to take her life just before he took his own. He understood Indian honor and their ways. She wondered how he learned. He seemed to be part Indian even with his white skin.

"Soon, we'll be home," Levi said. Will Forrester

pulled up spur-to-spur and grinned like a possum. He was still surprised they were alive and had their beaver pelts. They were as close to death as either man had ever been, even when the Comanche attacked them.

"I was ready to sing my death song back there— Dahteste was already singing." Will laughed. "I can't believe that cheeky bugger Hachta ended up with my stallion. If that doesn't take the cake. You just never know what's going to happen in the wilderness."

"It was a small price to pay to be saved, pard." Levi grinned and looked at his woman, then back at Forrester and added, "Yeah, you just never know."

A Look at Book Five:
The Old Dog: A Western Double

In the shadow of the high country, the hardest fight is with time.

The Old Dog

Back at the compound, Levi Johnson settles into life with his new wife, Dahteste—a Crow war chief whose presence stirs admiration, curiosity, and quiet tension among the mountain men. As Levi builds a home, Rusty Steel begins to question his place in a world that's moving on without him.

Feeling the pull of the wild and the bite of age, Rusty sets out alone to prove he still belongs in the mountains. A mysterious black dog joins him as he stalks a deadly mountain lion—and avoids becoming prey himself. But when smoke signals rise from the distant Crow camp, the time for reflection ends. Trouble is calling, and it won't wait.

Unforgotten

Captain Will Forrester rides out, searching for meaning in a world that's shifted beneath his boots. His closest friend is now married to a Crow warrior woman, and their shared vision of mountain life has split like a frostbitten trail. Alone, Will crosses paths with buffalo hunters seeking their fortune —and risking their lives in hostile lands.

As Will finds new footing and Levi navigates the delicate balance between two cultures, the compound braces for a storm of change. Old paths diverge, new dangers rise, and chaos sweeps through the mountains.

AVAILABLE OCTOBER 2025

ABOUT THE AUTHOR

 Ash Lingam was born and raised in Southern Ohio, not far from the mighty Ohio River. He had somewhat of an isolated upbringing on a family farm with his sisters. His best friends were his horse, Sugar, and his grandfather.

Born in 1886, the family patriarch grew crops, raised cattle, and doted on the young boy. At his grandfather's side, Ash learned about livestock and firearms at an early age. His grandad carried an old Colt with him at all times. It helped spawn a young boy's dreams of yesteryear.

Ash was only eight years old when his grandad taught him how to trap muskrats to prevent them from draining the farm's ponds. He gave him a double-barreled shotgun at twelve and taught him how to hunt to put food on the table.

It wasn't long before Ash was breaking horses. His spirited Tennessee Walker never allowed any other rider on her back. Together, they searched through the plowed fields in the spring, looking for Miami Indian arrowheads to add to his grandfather's ample collection.

Ash's family was among the early settlers in pre-

Revolutionary America. He has traced his lineage back to around 1746 when his ancestors immigrated from Europe to the aspiring American Colonies.

A retired marketing executive, Ash devotes his spare time to training police dogs and writing novels. He has found his niche in the Western, historical fiction, and adventure genres. With his vast vault of experience, he never runs out of sources for new stories. He has lived in eleven different countries and worked in a total of forty-six to date, Ash has written approximately 130 novels, short stories, and poems. More than one hundred of his eclectic titles help the American frontier come alive for his readers.

https://www.ashlingam.com/
Join the Lawless Waters Western Readers & Writers
Facebook Group